# Undamaged

No Rival #6

Charity Parkerson

I0667988

Without limiting the rights under copyright(s) reserved above and below, no part of this publication may be reproduced, stored in or introduced into a retrieval system, or transmitted, in any form, or by any means (electronic, mechanical, photocopying, recording, or otherwise) without the prior permission of the copyright owner.

### Please Note

The scanning, uploading, and distributing of this book via the internet or via any other means without the permission of the copyright owner is illegal and punishable by law. Criminal copyright infringement, including infringement without monetary gain, is investigated by the FBI and is punishable by up to 5 years in federal prison and a fine of $250,000. Please purchase only authorized electronic editions, and do not participate in or encourage electronic piracy of copyrighted materials. Brief passages may be quoted for review purposes if credit is given to the copyright holder. Your support of the author's rights is appreciated. Any resemblances to person(s) living or dead, is completely coincidental. All items contained within this novel are products of the author's imagination.

--Warning: This book is intended for readers over the age of 18.

Copyright © 2016 Charity Parkerson

Editor: Vicky Reese
This book was originally published by Ellora's Cave under the
same title.
ISBN-10: 1-946099-06-6
ISBN-13: 978-1-946099-06-8

All rights reserved.

No Rival series, book 6.

When Kip's boyfriend abandoned her,
Brian and Terry—two of MMA's greatest—
came to her rescue. Now, two years later,
they're the only ones who know the truth.
Kip has more dark secrets in her past than
just a no-good ex turned deadbeat dad.

Kip hadn't planned on staying in Vegas.
She'd thought to rest and move on—but
then, she hadn't expected to meet
someone like Cameron.

A horrific wartime injury changed
Cameron's mind and body. As part of
Terry's soldier rehabilitation program,
Cameron has fought his way back from
the brink. He's accepted he'll never regain
the life he once had but Kip makes him
dream.

When Kip's past threatens their fragile
love and tests the boundaries of all

Cameron stands for, he has to make a choice—give up the only person who makes him feel alive or embrace the fact there is no black and white.

# Dedication

For the world's best street team, The Naughty Crew. I couldn't function without you.

# Prologue

Kip and Cameron had met exactly twenty-two months ago. Yep. She'd taken to keeping life's score by months. She'd never even considered the concept until the day Kip learned she was pregnant. That day, everything changed. For nine months, she'd carried a new life inside her. Ten months, actually, but nobody told her that shit until it was too late. Everyone said nine months as if it was something cute, but forty weeks that had actually turned into forty-two was ten months and no one could tell Kip differently. She'd felt every minute of it.

Those ten months were the worst and greatest of Kip's life. No one could ever know why bringing her child into the world had been a mixture of heaven and hell for her. Brian and Terry had taken her in when she'd been at her lowest. Brian had been on tour, chasing the middleweight championship, when they met in Tennessee. From the very beginning, they'd been kindred spirits, watching their greatest loves slip away. Brian's life had worked out. Hers had not. Luckily, Brian and Terry had given her a soft place to land. They loved her and her daughter in spite of all the bad choices she'd made, but Cameron was the one who'd given Kip a reason to hope. His sexy laugh always took her breath. The way he watched her when he thought she wasn't looking tested every ounce of willpower she possessed. They'd known each other thirteen months and one week before Kip had noticed the hunger in his gaze each time he looked at her. Once she had, Kip couldn't look away. Pity he was a big fucking idiot who didn't know his worth.

# Chapter One

They were all hoping she'd get her top ripped off. Kip was no fool. She knew why the huge crowd pressed against the cage and the bets ran deep. The women's portion of the show was just that as far as this predominantly male crowd was concerned—a show. If she ever started doing this for them, it was time for her to quit. Her opponent, Tricia, was one of the toughest fighters at Warehouse District. That's exactly why Kip accepted her challenge. The pot was huge for such a bout but Kip didn't need the money. Not only did Terry refuse to broach the topic of her moving out, which would force her to support herself, even though they couldn't be together, Konstantin would never allow her to go without.

Tricia's first hit was direct. It landed

solidly against Kip's cheekbone, rocking her on her feet. For a moment, the room spun. The pain was surprisingly slow to follow. In a detached sort of way, Kip knew it was the adrenaline masking her agony. She also knew it wouldn't last forever. It was obvious the bleach-blonde behemoth wouldn't take mercy on Kip—not that she expected any leniency.

All she wanted was to last one full round and not make a fool of herself. With that goal in mind, Kip fell back on training and blocked out the crowd. One. Two. Breathe. She aimed for the woman's ribs, nearly crying out in relief when she connected before jumping backward. She wasn't quick enough. The air left Kip's lungs when her chest hit the mat and the blonde's ass landed in the center of Kip's spine. Before she had time to recover, a pain exploded through her shoulder. Her palm tapped the mat without her brain's permission. Well. Fuck. It went worse than expected, but she'd survived. At least she had her health.

Bouts between women were a new reality for Warehouse. Even though they'd given in to the demands for such matches, they hadn't gone out of their way to accommodate the fairer sex. Kip had easily accepted if she wanted to fight, she'd have to share a locker room with the men. Being raised in a combination of foster care homes and orphanages had toughened her skin against just this type of situation. Of course, the guys couldn't care less. Most were too pumped for their upcoming matches or riding the adrenaline high afterward. They paid little attention to their surroundings. Not that Kip was one to linger. Get in and get out. That was her motto, especially since losing didn't give her an overwhelming desire to chitchat. Unfortunately, Josh had other plans for her.

"You've been ignoring my phone calls."

Kip so wasn't in the mood for this tonight. Since most everyone believed Josh was Jade's father and Kip needed to keep it that way, she put her best face on. He could be tiresome some days. She eyed his blue Mohawk and the muscles bulging on her behalf. It really was too bad he was angry with her. "Hello to you too, Josh."

The locker next to her bowed beneath the force of his punch. He didn't move away. "I'm not fucking playing with you, Kipley. When I call, you pick up the goddamn phone. You owe me that much. I don't think you understand how difficult you're making things for me."

Because she knew it would piss him

off, Kip smirked. "Feel free to leave me in peace. No one will be surprised when you abandon me." Most people believed he was her ex and that he'd dumped her in Tennessee two years ago. She knew better.

His ice-blue gaze raked her body, leaving her chilled. He moved an inch closer. The bite of the cold locker hit her shoulder blades, stopping her retreat. One corner of his mouth lifted at her reaction.

"Who do you think would stop me if I carried you out of here? No one in this place would bat an eye. Your friends aren't here to step in."

Kip snorted. "Are you joking? You know there isn't a single move I make that Terry and Brian don't know about. They probably have half a dozen of their friends watching us right now."

Josh glanced around, obviously noting the eyes upon them. Instead of scaring him into stepping away, her words had the opposite effect. Leaning in, he hovered an inch from her face. An evil smile stretched his lips. "In that case we should give them a real show. Maybe it won't matter to Terry or Brian but I can think of at least one person who'd love to know all your secrets."

Cameron. Panic welled in Kip's chest. It was an empty threat. It had to be. Josh could never tell. She couldn't show him an ounce of weakness or he'd exploit it. She forced a chuckle to her lips. "I'm sure there're some people who would love to know all about you as well, Jozsua," she said, intentionally using his real name. "Do you think you're immune to public scorn?" Kip knew the moment the question left her lips she'd gone too far. She wanted to take it back.

His expression turned deadly. All

hint of an American accent was gone, replaced by a thick Russian she'd always been amazed he could keep hidden. "Don't play games with me, Kipley. Do you think Konstantin sent me here on a whim?"

Her blood froze. He was right. Konstantin had sent Josh to shadow her every move for a reason. He was vicious and deadly. Those were facts she needed to remember and she had to extricate herself from this position. There was bravery and then there was insanity. "Seriously, Josh," she said, keeping her voice level. "You know how stubborn I can be. I just—"

"Is there a problem here?"

Kip's gaze shot to the man hovering over Josh's shoulder. Kurt was one of the deadliest fighters at Warehouse. Everyone knew the man's reputation, including Josh. Of course, Josh wasn't one to be intimidated. There was fucked in the head like Kurt, and then there was been to hell and ruled like Josh. The difference wasn't subtle. Kurt would slaughter a man on the mat. With Josh, they may never find the body.

His gaze never left Kip's. "No problem at all. Isn't that right, Kipley?"

She gave a short nod. Not because she was scared but because Kurt was married to her boss and friend. Some things cut too deep for Kip to share. Josh was one of those things. He was a constant reminder of a different time—one she couldn't forget.

"We'll pick up this conversation later, eh? Answer the damn phone."

Kipley nodded again. Josh held her stare for a moment longer, ensuring she understood he meant for her to obey. Pushing away from the lockers, he shouldered his way past Kurt without a backward glance. She didn't release the breath she hadn't known she was holding until he was out of sight.

"What was all that about?"

Grabbing her bag, Kip avoided Kurt's searching gaze. "Nothing."

"Do you need someone to walk you out?"

The concern in Kurt's voice was almost her undoing. Her insides shook. She hated when Josh was pissed at her but she equally hated when he wasn't. The guilt was all on her because Kip couldn't say any of that. Instead, she drew on the dregs of her inner strength and flashed Kurt a smile she didn't feel. "I'm good. Seriously. Josh was being Josh. It's nothing to worry about."

"Josh being Josh sounds like something to worry about to me but hey, you're a big girl, right?"

"Right," Kip agreed. Even to her it sounded like a complete fucking lie.

* * * * *

Her shoulders hurt like hell. Pain made Kip weepy. Crying always led to weakness. Those moments always ended with Konstantin. Sometimes it only took the sound of his voice to steady Kip. Thank God, since that's all she had.

"I miss you." The admission alone loosened a bit of tightness in her chest.

"I miss you, my Kipley."

His deep Russian accent brushed her skin, causing chill bumps to rise on her arms.

It didn't matter it was more familiar to her than anyone around her. She never tired of listening to him speak.

"It's bad tonight, Konstantin. Worse than usual. It's like a stone sitting on my chest and glass in my gut." He was a sickness and she didn't care if he knew.

"Say the word and I'll send for you."

There was a long pause, making her wish for the millionth night in a row that things were different. There'd been so many times she'd almost caved. The only thing that saved her was the sure knowledge it would be a temporary high and the lows were too low. "The heart can only take so much," Kip whispered.

"It sits on my chest," Konstantin said, tearing at her soul. As much as she'd always needed him to feel the same, she'd never wanted him to hurt. "But you don't want this life."

There was always a "but" with Konstantin and the pain in his voice let her know it was true. She'd never fully understood what the world was like in Russia. There'd always been only their life here. At eighteen, she'd fallen in love with Konstantin Danshov at first sight. The Russian-born hockey player's hard body and sky-blue eyes had swept her off her feet. But there'd been another side of him. A side she hadn't known about it until it was too late. This dark side of drug trafficking and mafia ties had ended in his deportation and she'd been left alone. While most people would label him an evil man, she knew better. No one could convince her otherwise. She'd seen him in a different light and no one knew him the way Kip did.

"I crave you, Kipley. Every day. Underneath me and moaning my name."

"I want you too." It was the only response she could drum up. Sometimes, at her weakest, she wondered how much more of this her mind could withstand.

A humming noise came from the

back of Konstantin's throat. The deep vibration hardened her nipples as always. She'd felt that sound on her skin before. It meant pleasure was soon to follow. Kip snuggled deeper into the mattress. Her eyes fell closed. An image of Konstantin flared to life in her mind. His massive frame surrounded her, making her feel safe and arousing her beyond reason. Konstantin's body was a weapon, honed to perfection and built to take a hit. She missed the sensation of hard muscles beneath her palms. The memory of it dampened her panties. When she spoke, Kip didn't bother hiding her arousal. No one would judge her. "Sometimes my body aches in the absence of yours."

Konstantin drew an unsteady breath. The sound always made her wonder if he was touching himself. She'd watched his face as he'd made that exact noise thousands of times. He was so fucking sexy in the throes of passion. When he stroked his cock, every hard line came to life, straining toward orgasm.

"I'm only content when your juices are coating every inch of my skin." She knew it was true. He was pleasure in excess.

"The way your skin tastes as you come against my lips is the most addictive flavor in the world. Press your palm against your mound, Kip, and listen to my voice. Let me pretend for a little while it's me."

Slipping her hand inside her panties, Kip did as he asked. A knock landed on her bedroom door, drawing a growl from her lips. A low chuckle stroked her ear. She missed his next words when Cameron's voice sounded through the door.

"Hey, Kip. It's Cameron."

Konstantin's voice rumbled in her ear, pulling her attention back his way. "Let him take care of you, Kipley. I can't be there with you. Don't shut him out. I love you, my angel."

Konstantin fell silent. The face of her phone went black. With a sad sigh, she tossed it aside.

"Come in."

Cameron slipped inside the room, pulling the door closed behind him. When he spotted her tucked beneath the covers, he hesitated. Kip rolled to her side. She stared at him while barely resisting the urge to laugh at his obvious discomfort. Intentionally she did nothing to ease it.

"I wanted to check on you after your fight." He glanced at his watch. "I didn't expect to find you in bed."

She threw back the covers and sat

up, revealing her spaghetti-strap shirt and panties. Cameron cleared his throat. It was an uncomfortable sound.

"Maybe I'll come back in the morning."

He looked adorably unsure of himself and sexy as sin. Before meeting him, Kip had no idea a police uniform could be so delicious. An inner sigh ran through her head. Another hard body to lead her to perdition.

"It's fine. I was sulking."

An unexpected smile exploded across Cameron's face even as he visibly fought to keep his eyes locked on hers. "Got your ass handed to you, huh?"

She shrugged, purposely allowing one strap to fall from her shoulder, exposing the top of her breast. For a second, Cameron's gaze dropped before meeting hers once again.

"We both knew I would. I can't say it wouldn't have been nice to win but it wasn't about that."

Shoving his hands into his pockets, Cameron leaned his shoulders against the closed door behind him. "What was it about then?"

She shrugged again, making the strap slide farther down her arm. "Pride. I've been training for so long now, I needed to prove I could last at least one full round against someone as vicious as Tricia."

His gaze moved over her face. "You'll have a black eye tomorrow."

He was too far away. This need to have him closer had nothing to do with the adrenaline high she'd been on earlier in the night. Nor did it have anything to do with Konstantin's voice still ringing in her ears. Cameron had been a genuine weakness for Kip since they met.

"I don't bite. That's a lie," she added before he tested her theory. "I totally do bite but that's no reason for you to be scared."

A hint of challenge flashed in Cameron's gaze. Even though both his eyes were blue, one was a shade lighter than the other. They were gorgeous and mesmerizing.

"For all you know, I like that," he said, pushing away from the wall.

She gave the spot next to her a pat.

His mouth lifted in one corner. "Do you promise not to pounce?"

Kip couldn't have stopped the evil smile from pulling at her lips if she tried. "No."

He was across the room in a flash. Cameron didn't accept her offer to sit. Instead, her back hit the mattress as he covered her body with his. Their mouths clashed—hot and hard. They'd kissed before but this time there was something feral about him.

Cameron shifted positions, cupping her breast. His thumb brushed her nipple. "Why do you tease me?" he asked between kisses.

It was a fair question. If his tongue wasn't so fucking delicious, she might have answered right away. As it was, she waited until he pulled away.

"I'm never teasing. You just refuse to take me seriously for some reason."

With his lips swollen from her kisses and the flush of arousal on his cheeks, Kip was having a hard time not attacking him. His expression kept her in check. He didn't believe her. She wanted to growl. Cameron came home from Afghanistan half-dead and with extensive scarring down one side of body after he'd thrown himself on top of an Afghani child who'd been set on fire in the street. The boy hadn't survived. Sometimes she didn't think Cameron truly had either. The scarring didn't take away from his sexiness at all but she'd always known that, in his mind, it did. He was eyeing her with suspicion. She hated it.

"Kurt tells me Josh showed up at Warehouse District tonight."

Once again, he'd avoided her advances. Picking a fight was his favorite ploy. She made a valiant attempt to push her way out from beneath him without luck.

"Tattletale." Kip was incapable of keeping the bitterness from her tone.

"Tell me what he wanted."

She pushed again but Cameron refused to budge. Giving up, she sighed. "Nothing."

"Kurt said you told him the same thing, but according to him it looked like something."

"It's nothing I can't handle."

Kip wondered for a minute if Cameron would shake her in his frustration. "You shouldn't go to Warehouse alone. It's a rough place. Anything could happen to you."

"I wasn't alone."

Cameron ignored her protest. "Josh isn't right in the head."

Kip locked her back teeth together. Every secret she kept tasted heavy on her tongue but she refused to allow them to fall. In her wildest dreams, Kip couldn't have seen this coming. When she and Josh had very publicly parted ways in Tennessee, she'd been five months pregnant. Brian and Terry had taken her in. It had never been her intention to involve anyone in her bullshit. Yet here they were.

"Come on, Kip. You can talk to me. Does he want you back? Is he planning to fight you for custody of Jade? Tell me what's going on so I can help."

She wanted to. "I can't."

"Are you afraid of him?"

A burst of irritation ran through her. Cameron needed to let this go. "No." Kip barely stopped herself from growling. "He'd only think to put his hands on me once but he never would," she added, in case Cameron thought her answer meant Josh might.

Her claim didn't seem to have any effect on Cameron. He continued searching her gaze as if looking for holes in her claim.

"Has he ever hit you?"

Kip snorted again. Konstantin

would've seen him dead. "I'm being serious, Kip. I've seen Josh snap before."

If only it had been anyone else questioning her, Kip might have held her temper. Cameron's opinion mattered. Obviously, he thought of her as a helpless female—one who made terrible decisions.

"For fuck's sake, Cameron. I can handle Josh. This was a one-time thing. He won't come near me again."

"Kip..." Oh, she hated that condescending tone on his gorgeous lips. "He's Jade's father. You'll have to deal with that eventually. As much as I don't like the guy, he has rights. He could go after them in court."

A growl ripped from her throat. She hated it with a desperate passion when people lectured her. Her anger finally gave her the strength needed to shove her way from underneath his weight. She didn't bother to cover herself as she headed for the door. Throwing it wide, she motioned toward the hall. "I think it's time for you to go." She really didn't want him to leave but he would not stop. His determination to know everything was almost tangible.

Cameron ran his hands through his hair, leaving it standing on end. He couldn't have looked more frustrated or sexy but Kip was done with men pushing her around for the night.

"Damn it, Kip. I'm trying to help. If you think Josh is a danger to you or Jade, then let me help you."

As much as Kip would've liked to believe that passion drove her in that moment, she couldn't lie to herself. She was simply tired. Life left her fucking exhausted and she couldn't work up the energy to care what he thought of her any longer. Secrets weighed more than carrying sand bags around 24/7.

"I'm sorry you think I'm such a shit mother that I would allow my pride to stand in the way if I thought for a second Jade was in danger. This thing with Josh has nothing to do with her."

Cameron came to his feet. "I don't think you're a shit mother. You're an amazing mom. Josh will eventually take this to court even if only in an attempt to get you back. He'd have to be crazy not to use every weapon he could to keep you at his side. If I was in his shoes, I'd do everything in my power to force you to come back to me."

She reacted before she could stop herself. Kip stamped her foot. She'd been coming on to Cameron for too long and had been shut down too many times. It pissed her off that he obviously felt something for her but he held back. She was shattered from fighting for every inch. She was just damn tired period. Life pissed her off. "He won't take me to court, Cameron. Now. Get the hell out."

Kip could see it in his expression. He didn't understand what he'd done to anger her. Why did he have to care about her? It made everything so much harder to bear. She sighed. "Look. You obviously don't want me and I have no desire to fight anyone else tonight."

Total silence met her claim. A muscle in Cameron's jaw ticked. "I want you."

There wasn't an ounce of emotion in his tone but he meant it. Damn. It hurt.

"No, Cameron. You don't. Maybe you desire me in a physical way but you don't want me. You don't even know me, not really, and I don't want to do this any longer." It was a total lie. He meant more

34

to her the he could ever know.

"Look, Kip," Cameron began, sounding as tired as she felt. "You need to put a stop to this. Josh should be paying child support, or signing his rights away. I don't understand why you're letting him get away with this unless he's threatening you in some way."

"Damn it, Cameron. Josh isn't Jade's father." Kip wanted to bite off her tongue, but once the confession was out there, hanging between them, she couldn't stop. "I was already pregnant when I started dating Josh and he knew it."

Cameron looked as if she'd slapped him. He opened his mouth, obviously intent on saying more. Terry appeared in the doorway, saving her from making things worse. He eyed them both, seemingly oblivious to her state of undress and Cameron's rage. His gaze lingered on

Kip's face and she knew he saw it all. The man always knew everything. It was as maddening as it was endearing. A flash of sympathy crossed his features before he focused on Cameron.

"You're going to wake up Jade."

With a sharp nod, Cameron came to his feet. His emotions were on lockdown. Kip swore the temperature in the room dropped by ten degrees.

"We're not through discussing this," Cameron promised.

She couldn't let him leave believing she'd tell him anything more. "Yes. We are. This is none of your business."

Cameron's face hardened in a way she'd never witnessed before. He was done with her. She could feel their bond being cut. She wanted to throw her arms wide and scream but she knew no amount of yelling could match the pitch inside her head as he left. Kip didn't miss the fact that Terry's lips were pressed into a hard line before he followed the other man down the hall. There was no way she was getting out of talking to him about this later. With a growl, Kip threw on the first pair of shorts she could find and headed in the opposite direction of the men. Maybe if she was quiet, no one would look for her for a while. As she hit the back door, she switched on the intercom for Jade's bedroom. If Jade woke up, Kip didn't want to miss it. Her chest hurt. Some days, she wanted to take her daughter and run. There was nothing holding her to this town...except all the people she'd come to love. Fuck. If there was one thing Kip knew how to do, it was totally back herself into a corner.

\* \* \* \* \*

*"Your eyes are very green."*

*They pressed their foreheads together, attempting to see into each other's eyes as closely as possible.*

*A laugh escaped Kip before she could call it back. "Your eyes are very blue."*

*Konstantin's low chuckle brushed her skin with the lightest of touches. "Imagine how beautiful our babies will be."*

The oversized hammock swayed, jerking Kip from her memories. Terry climbed in next to her. She automatically shifted to make room for him and curled into his side. With her head on his chest, she could hear the steady beating of his heart. He was such a stable and strong man. No wonder Brian had been completely lost to him the moment they met.

"Have you ever needed anyone, Kip?"

*I love you, my Kipley.*

"Yes." Even to Kip her voice came out sounding small.

Terry's arms tightened around her. "Have you ever needed me? I mean, I know you've never really needed me financially. For the life of me, I've never been able to figure out why you've stayed."

"My heart needs you," she answered without having to think about it. It was true she had needed no one to support her. Konstantin would never allow her to want for anything. "Cameron's not likely to ever forgive me."

Terry was silent for so long she didn't think he would respond. When he did, his words came out haltingly as if he measured each one.

"I don't think he's ever met anyone like you. He's just trying to get his bearings. On one hand, he hopes to save you. On the other, he'd like to throttle you."

Kip snorted at the heavy laughter in Terry's voice. "But all the rest of him just wants to be with you."

The night wind caused a ripple across the pool's water. Kip couldn't tear her eyes away from it as she mulled over Terry's claim. She thought at least half of his statement was true but she wasn't sure which half. Gah! It was hardly Cameron's fault she was a fucked-up mess.

"I owe you my life. That's a debt I can never repay," Terry said so quietly she might've missed his words if her ear hadn't been resting on his chest.

"Are you feeling maudlin or trying to distract me from my self-pity?"

Terry snorted at her question. "Neither. It just occurs to me I've never said that to you."

It had been two years since Terry had nearly died from non-Hodgkin's lymphoma. No one looking at him today could tell that the heart currently beating against her cheek had stopped only yards from where they lay.

"Some would say Konstantin is owed that debt. All I did was make a call."

"How much did that cost him? If nothing else, I'd like to repay any money he spent on my behalf."

Terry had been given a death sentence. He'd needed an experimental drug not yet approved by the FDA. He'd been put on a waiting list but his time had been short. The list had not. Konstantin had pulled some strings, shooting Terry to the top of the list and saving his life. Kip would make that call a thousand times. Some people might see what she did as wrong. She didn't give a fuck.

"You lived. Your debt is paid."

She felt him tense and she knew her answer wasn't enough. "There has to be something I can do."

Kip wrapped her arm tighter around his waist and held on. Terry did not understand how much his life meant to her. Having someone in the world who knew all her secrets and still cared what happened to her, that was a rare thing. Another strong breeze unsettled the water. The rippling effect was hypnotic.

*It was hot as hell and the water was calling her name. Picking up the pace, Kip rounded the corner. Pain exploded up her leg as her little toe connected with the two-hundred-year-old antique table Konstantin kept at the top of the stairs. "Goddamn it!" Hopping on one leg, Kip tried to alleviate* the pain. "Ow! Motherfucker."

Konstantin's huge frame shook the floor as he came stampeding from the bedroom. For someone who stood over six feet and was three hundred pounds of solid muscle, the man was fast on his feet. He skidded to a stop at her side.

"What's happened? Where are you hurt?"

Konstantin's adorable, overprotective nature wasn't even enough to calm her anger. She freaking hated to hurt herself.

"I think I broke my toe on that stupid fucking table."

Sitting down on the top step, she tried inspecting the damage. A shadow passed overhead a split second before a loud crash echoed off the walls. Kip stared in horror at the splintered table now lying at the foot of the stairs. Her mouth fell open.

*Before she had time to recover, the coat rack that usually sat beside the table went next. It flew out in an arc, seeming to hang midair for a moment before crashing down beside the table. A lamp went next. By the time Kip flew to her feet, Konstantin was poised to throw a plant.*

*"What in the hell are you doing?"*

*His face was set in a hard line. "Nothing hurts my baby." She blinked. He threw the plant.*

*"But…" she stuttered, foot forgotten. "What did the plant do?"*

*"Nothing yet," he answered, searching the area with his gaze as if looking for his next victim. "I'm not taking any chances."*

*His gaze landed on a trunk that had been passed down from his grandmother's mother. Panic welled in her chest. He took two steps in its direction.*

44

*"No, Kon. Don't do it."* He outweighed her by nearly two hundred pounds but she still tried wrapping herself around him like a monkey. *"Please? Stop."*

*As if she weighed nothing, Konstantin plucked her off his side and slung her up into his arms. His gorgeous eyes locked on her face. The concern written in every line of his face made her heart turn over.*

*"I'll stop smashing shit when you promise me you'll never hurt again."*

*Her nose stung. Damn. She loved this man. "You know I can't promise I'll never hurt."*

*He set her down and headed for the trunk. Without a single thought, she jumped on his back.*

*"No, Kon."*

*He pretended to go down underneath her weight, falling to one knee while still somehow shifting her into his arms. Her back touched the floor. Konstantin's palms were braced on either side of her head. His laughing gaze met hers.*

*"Promise me, baby. Say the words."*

*Her mouth went dry as his weight leaned into her until she was cradling his hips at the apex of her thighs. There was nothing she wouldn't do for him. "I swear I'll never hurt again."*

Kip blinked back tears and rubbed her cheek against Terry's chest. "You lived. I smiled. Trust me, Konstantin was paid in full."

# Chapter Two

"*Měla byses dostat ven častěji.*"

"I have no desire to go out more." Kip didn't bother looking away from her magazine as she responded to Kurt's observation.

"I knew it!"

That got her attention. She blinked at Kurt, doing her best to decipher his triumphant tone. "I was under the impression you knew a lot of things. You'll have to be more specific."

"You were reading Franz Kafka earlier."

Kip's confusion grew. "Okay," she said, drawing out the last syllable.

She didn't even know where to begin asking questions. McKenna and Kurt were hard work when it came to conversations. They made her brain hurt. Since they signed her paycheck, Kip did her best to keep up. Thankfully, the bookstore where she shook a cash register all day also served coffee. The smell alone kept her on her toes—except for moments like now. The store was dead. Kurt had too much time on his hands.

"You understood me."

Realization dawned. He'd been testing her. "Ah. Kafka writes in German. You spoke Czech so I don't see your point."

"My point is that you don't get out often enough."

She opened her mouth to protest or remind him one had nothing to do with the other, but it seemed he wasn't finished.

"Lucky for you I know exactly who can help you with that."

As if they'd practiced ahead of time and had been waiting for their cue, Max and Ryan appeared out of nowhere. Ryan wore a luminous smile, dimples and all, while Max's grin was wicked. It dripped with the promise of sexual satisfaction. Kip barely resisted the urge to fan her face.

Max and Ryan owned a fitness center where they also taught self-defense classes. The men did an amazing amount of business. Kip secretly believed women signed up in droves, hoping to get pinned to the floor by one or both of the men. She knew it was why she'd signed up. Unfortunately for all the women of the world, Max and Ryan were most decidedly gay and in love with each other. But their sexual preference didn't lessen their impact on a woman's girlie bits one iota.

"You should definitely come out and play with us, Kip."

She forcibly stamped down her inner tramp at the sound of Ryan's sexy voice. It was hard but Kip kept her drooling to a minimum.

"Be honest. The three of you practiced this skit for a week, didn't you?"

One corner of Max's mouth lifted and his eyes took on a mischievous glint. Kip blushed. Dear lord. It wasn't fair. There was no way she could hide the way he affected her.

"Practice makes perfect, as they say, and we're damn close. Ryan's right. You should come."

Only the fact she'd already been leaning on the counter saved her ass. Her knees weakened. Both men were equal in height, coming in around six feet. Even though Kip was short, she didn't doubt her ability to climb either man should they decide to switch teams. Kurt's knowing chuckle stopped her from embarrassing herself.

"I have a daughter, so as much as

I'd love to come..." And she really would, in more ways than one. "I'll have to pass."

Kurt waved away her words. "Jade is having a sleepover with Tayrn tonight." Damn. Apparently, McKenna had been plotting against her. Kurt and McKenna's daughter was only a few months older than Jade, and even though they were still toddlers the pair were already inseparable. It was exactly the sort of life she'd wanted for her daughter—friends and normalcy. A life she'd never had. The thought tightened her throat as an image of Cameron sprang to mind. Two years... They'd been friends for a whole twenty-two months. Damn, she hated losing him.

With a heavy sigh, Kip did the only thing she could. She gave in gracefully.

"Fine. I'll fucking go and act like a fucking grown-up for a couple of fucking hours." Well. It sounded graceful in her head.

* * * * *

To give Cameron credit, he appeared every bit as surprised to see her as Kip was to see him. It was Ryan and Max she couldn't get a read on. Kip imagined it was common knowledge—among the gossips in their tiny MMA family—that she and Cameron had argued. Until recently, she hadn't thought of the pair as busybodies. However, as the men's destination came into view, Kip's steps faltered. There were hundreds of people inside Hal's Dance Hall and Saloon.

Cameron stood out from the rest, sitting alone at a corner table and tilting back a longneck. Sheesh. He was as sexy as sin—in and out of uniform. The soft gray t-shirt he wore strained across his chest. Hungry stares watched him from every direction. Kip knew the exact moment he noticed her. It was obvious he caught sight of Ryan first. A smile stretched his lips. That is until Cameron's gaze shifted. Their eyes met. Cameron's smile fell. His disappointment at seeing her there hurt. She couldn't lie. Sometimes it sucked being an independent woman. What Kip really wanted to do was stamp her foot in frustration...or kick Cameron in the balls.

He had done nothing wrong, per se, but it wouldn't kill him to take one for his team. They'd been demolishing the female side for years. Ever the gentleman, he stood when they reached the table. The bastard even pulled out a chair for her to sit. Kip smiled in thanks. At least she hoped she did. In truth, her expression felt like a grimace. When Cameron reclaimed his seat, he leaned away from her. Kip saw it happen out of the corner of her eye. To keep from tearing up, she focused on the dance floor, not really seeing a thing. With her mind locked firmly on ignoring Cameron, Kip nearly jumped out of her skin when his fingertips skimmed her forearm. Her gaze shot to his.

"I'm sorry," she said automatically.

The frown pulling at his brow cleared away at her apology. "Ryan asked you three times if you'd like something to drink."

"I'm sorry," she repeated, sort of wanting to bite off her own tongue. "I was..." Kip had no idea how to finish that sentence.

One corner of his mouth lifted. "Pretending I'm not here," he finished for her.

"I'd love something," she said, avoiding the truth in his statement. "But I can get it myself."

"Of course you can," Cameron muttered, sounding disappointed as he looked away.

Thankfully, Ryan saved her from issuing a third apology.

"Babe, I didn't ask if you could get a drink. I asked if you wanted one. Now you'll take whatever I give you as a way to make it up to me." He dropped his chin and gave his best puppy-dog eyes. "You wouldn't want to hurt my feelings, would you?"

Before she had time to respond, a glass filled to the brim with milky liquid appeared in front of her.

"White Russian." The man who'd set the drink on the table let his fingers linger over the glass for a moment before moving away.

Kip's pulse beat in her ears as her eyes moved upward until colliding with his ice- blue stare. The brim of the straw cowboy hat he wore was tugged low, hiding his blue Mohawk and casting a shadow over a majority of his face. It didn't matter because Kip knew his every line. A slow smile stretched his lips until full-on dimples and gleaming white teeth shook Kip from her shock.

"She's not drinking anything we didn't watch the bartender pour," Cameron barked, surprising Kip with his anger.

She couldn't tear her gaze away from Josh hovering over her long enough to see if Cameron's expression matched his tone. The saddened eyes holding her captive never left hers.

"May I have this dance?"

Kip barely stopped herself from glancing at Cameron to seek permission. That ridiculous thought had her setting her hand inside the one offered to her. As Josh's fingers enclosed hers, Kip wondered if her knees would support her when she stood, in light of his earlier anger. Not that he gave her time to test them out. With the slightest tug, he had her on her feet and moving toward the dance floor. His arms encircled her waist the second they hit its edge. As Kip's palms slid up his chest and around his neck, her fingers automatically sought the soft hairs at his nape. She didn't draw an easy breath until she felt them. He was really there and he didn't look pissed or anything. The scent of spicy cologne tickled her nose. She inhaled the aroma into her lungs.

"I can't believe you're here after the way our last conversation went."

"Don't be stupid. I never stay mad for long. You look beautiful tonight." The pride in his voice had her blinking back tears but her throat refused to work.

"What the fuck are you doing, Kip?"

Ignoring the irritation in his voice, she pressed her cheek to his chest, hoping to feel his heart beating against her ear. Heartbeats were her Kryptonite. They reminded her she wasn't alone. With the soothing vibration caressing her senses, Kip chose to play dumb. "I'm dancing with you."

He sighed. A smile pulled at her lips.

"You know what I mean. Konstantin wouldn't want this for you."

Ouch. Low blow. Still, she didn't intend to cave so easily. "I disagree. Konstantin would love to see us dancing like this. He was always a visual beast."

Josh pinched her ass. When she jumped in surprise, his touch turned into a caress. "Quit playing the fool. You're allowing life to turn you bitter."

It was true. That didn't mean she had to admit it. "I'm out with friends. Bitter people don't do things like that."

"I'm aware."

Kip smiled against his chest. "See? I'm not bitter."

Josh's low laugh was like music to her ears even though there was nothing nice about the sound.

"We could disappear, you know? It would be as if we never existed."

To hide the longing in her eyes, Kip kept her cheek pressed to his chest, absorbing his strength. She could never tell him how many times she'd considered doing just that. "Except we do."

He set his chin on her head and his grip tightened. "Yeah, I know, but you should have a normal life with a man who comes home to you and Jade every night.

What about this guy who's eyeing us as if he wants to rip out my spine?"

"You know Cameron."

"That's not what I meant."

She knew what he meant but hoped to avoid the topic. For a moment, she felt at peace. Nothing about the way she felt for Cameron was peaceful. It was deep longing and bottomless yearning. It was ugly and messy because everything in her life was that way.

"He kind of hates me right now."

"Idiot."

Kip smiled at the annoyance in Josh's tone. "Love you."

He pressed his lips to the top of her head at the declaration and whispered into her hair. "Love you too. Let's go give the cop a reason to be pissed."

*

"Whoa. We recognize that look," Ryan

said, snagging Cameron's attention.

Cameron touched the longneck to his lips to buy some time. Ryan and Max's knowing gazes crawled over his skin. With nothing left to keep him from responding, Cameron went with avoidance.

"I have no idea what you're talking about."

A ghost of a smile passed over Max's lips, ensuring Cameron knew he wasn't fooling anyone with his denial. Ryan wasn't as subdued.

"Please. Spare me. Do you have any idea how many nights we've staked out the wares together?"

"And again," Cameron stressed. "I have no idea where you're going with this."

"Well, let's see," Ryan said, working up to a real show. He tossed one arm across the back of Max's chair while settling deeper into his. "We both know you want Kip."

Cameron spent a moment debating the merits of arguing before deciding he couldn't force out that lie. When he didn't call Ryan a liar, the man continued.

"Now in comes this guy. I mean, dear lord, look at him. I have to admit, as many times as I've seen Josh, I've never really looked at him, because let's be honest, he doesn't invite the eye with his surly-ass attitude but damn... That's one big bastard. His arms are the size of my thighs. Kip is snuggling in pretty close there. Seriously it's obvious they've met before."

"And fucked," Max added, throwing in his two cents.

"And fucked," Ryan agreed. "But here's the thing..."

A wicked smile touched Ryan's lips. Dread ate at Cameron's gut.

"While you've been busy watching them, we've been busy watching you. Would you like to know what we've seen?"

No. He really wouldn't but he could see they would not be deterred.

"You're so fucking jealous you can't see straight."

Cameron's mind went blank. He cleared his throat, hoping against hope he could survive this conversation with his reputation intact. "I'm not jealous. There's nothing going on between Kip and me."

Max snorted. "That's bullshit and you know it. You've got a whole hell of a lot going on with that little girl."

Ryan kept Cameron from having to issue a second denial. "You, my friend, are in luck. You have us."

"How is that lucky for me?"

Their matching evil grins did nothing to comfort him.

"Because when it comes to luring someone to join us in bed, we're the grand master chiefs of debauchery."

If there was one thing Cameron could cling to in order to save his ass, it was the truth. He prided himself on spotting a liar or fraud a mile away. Ryan was being one hundred percent honest. Of course, Cameron had heard rumors over the years. He'd assumed—incorrectly, it seemed—those things had gone down in the days when the pair had been hiding from their feelings for each other. Now it seemed to Cameron as if Ryan was insinuating this was something they still did.

The realization was almost funny. Before that moment, Cameron had never thought of himself as gossipy. As he leaned forward in his seat, going as far as to set his elbows on the table to be closer to the pair, Cameron realized he simply had to know. Ryan and Max's evil smiles grew at the move since it was more than apparent they'd snagged him.

"I do believe we should extend an invitation to a particular club to our friends, Max," Ryan said mischievously.

Max nodded. "Agreed. I think Cameron and Kip would be very cozy joining us in a private room at a certain underground locale."

The Sahara Desert magically appeared, taking up shop right between Cameron's brain and tongue. It was the only excuse he could muster for how completely his thoughts dried up, leaving him with nothing in the aftermath of Max's statement. Cameron knew the club they referred to. This couldn't be good. Kip and Josh arrived at the edge of the table, saving him from having to respond.

"Everyone has met Josh, right?" she asked, motioning in the man's direction.

Ryan and Max shook Josh's hand and shuffled around to make room. Josh seemed different tonight—more subdued. Less hardened by life. Cameron couldn't put his finger on it. It didn't matter. He still wanted to break both the man's legs. The extra person at the table had Kip pressed closer to Cameron's side than before. Because he couldn't help himself, he draped his arm across the back her chair, staking his claim. Josh's mouth lifted in one corner. Fucker. He'd owned the world when he'd had Kip and had thrown it away. Cameron would be damned if Josh got it back. The more Cameron thought about it, the more it pissed him off. Leaning over, he spoke against Kip's ear, making sure no one else could hear.

"Doesn't want you back, huh? Want to tell me another one?"

She didn't as much as glance in his direction, but Kip being Kip, she found another way to have her revenge. She lifted the drink Josh had brought her to her lips. Cameron growled. Truly. The sound rumbled from the back of his throat. Kip smirked.

"I wish you wouldn't drink that, Kip."

Everyone was watching, waiting to see what she'd do—except Josh. He was challenging Cameron with his stare, daring him to say anything else. The testosterone was enough to choke everyone at the table. Kip shrugged as if oblivious to it all.

"I can't get anyone to take advantage of me sober. Maybe a little roofie sex is just what the doctor ordered."

Without giving Cameron time to respond, she tipped up the glass and chugged its contents.

Ryan threw back his head, roaring with laughter. He swiped at his eyes. "Damn. I like you."

Kip wiped her mouth and flashed him a grateful smile. "The feeling is mutual." Cameron wanted to be pissed. Josh's expression gave Cameron pause. The man should've appeared triumphant since he'd won this round. Instead, Josh simply held Cameron's stare and looked resigned.

"Did you really think I'd drug Kip? Harsh."

Josh stood and pressed his lips to Kip's cheek, saying something only she could hear. When she nodded, he straightened away and dipped his chin at them.

"Later." He walked away, heading straight for a curvy brunette at the bar.

Cameron stared at Kip's profile, searching for any sign she felt anything at all—jealousy, remorse, or anger. There was nothing. Kip cared about Josh, that much was obvious by watching the pair, but not in the way Cameron had believed. Watching them interact was...odd. Of course, this newfound knowledge also meant he was an ass for constantly picking that fight with her. It also didn't change the fact that Josh was always around, showing up everywhere Kip went. Josh's every action smacked too much of stalking.

"Would you like another drink?"

Kip's gaze shot to his as if surprised to find him speaking to her. "No thank you."

"Come on, Kip. You have to have

another drink. You'll need fortification for the night we have planned."

Ryan's claim snagged Kip's attention. Cameron hated the loss of her stare. He also wasn't too happy about her refusal to give him an inch.

A nervous-sounding chuckle left her lips. It was obvious he wasn't the only one who'd heard the rumors about Ryan and Max. That thought had Cameron leaning even closer to Kip. Had she heard the tales? If so, why had she still chosen to come out with the pair tonight? Damn. She kept him chasing her intentions.

"Um," she said, eyes skirting away. "What exactly are our plans for the evening?"

Max leaned forward in his chair, focusing on Kip with barely contained fire. The change in him was enthralling. It was obvious Kip wasn't immune. Her lips parted and a flush rose on her cheeks. Cameron swiped his fingers over his mouth to hide his smile. This should be good. Even he couldn't look away from the wicked glint in Max's eyes.

"This place is a bit loud. We were thinking of moving this party to a quieter location."

Kip shocked him by not backing down. "I'm guessing you know just the place."

"Oh yeah." The challenge in Max's gaze couldn't be missed.

"I think I'll take that drink now."

The laugh rumbling from Max's chest could only be described as depraved. If the promise of sexual pleasure had a sound, it had just fallen from Max's lips. "Drink fast. We have other places to be."

Cameron and Kip were literally fucked.

* * * * *

Even though Kip had arrived at Hal's with Max and Ryan, she agreed to ride with Cameron when they left. He stared at the taillights of Ryan's truck, picturing all the terrible turns this night could take as he ignored the deafening silence inside his car. If Kip was as much as breathing, he couldn't tell.

He couldn't take any more. "Are you going to stay mad at me forever?"

"I'm not mad."

The blatant lie had him glancing her way. He expected her to avoid his gaze.

Instead, he found her staring at him. His lips pulled at the corners without his permission. Because it was Kip, he knew exactly how to respond. "I'm not sorry for caring too much."

A smile exploded across her face. "I'm not sorry for wanting you and not a savior." As far as apologies went, they'd pulled it off beautifully to Cameron's way of thinking. Ryan's blinker flashed and Cameron followed, turning into Arden Fair mall.

All the shops were closed this time of night but they weren't going there. They were headed underground. As they stepped from the car, Kip looked around. It was obvious she was curious but she wouldn't ask. He knew her too well. She was the most independent person he'd ever met. She'd never back down from an open challenge. Max and Ryan flanked them on either side, making Cameron feel as if he was being escorted to perdition. The nondescript building gave no hint of the debauchery taking place just below the surface.

When a dark-haired man stepped from the shadows, Kip started a little at

Cameron's side. There was nothing about the man that would make him stand out in a crowd. He was average height, average build and had average looks. He was exactly like thousands of people Cameron saw on a daily basis. The man nodded at Max even though his expression held. There was no judgment. Still, Cameron couldn't get inside and out from beneath the man's stare fast enough. With a quick scan of his keycard, the doorman let them inside, and Max led the way down a darkened staircase. A soft light shone at the bottom and low music floated up the stairs. The farther they went the more the temperature dropped. Cameron bit back a laugh. He'd expected hell to be warmer.

As the first moan reached his ears, Cameron barely stopped himself from glancing behind him to see Kip's reaction. He had to admit there'd been a tiny part of him that hoped he was wrong about where they were headed. If the noises surrounding them weren't enough to tell the tale, the sheer curtains allowing them a clear view of a few of the blatant sexual acts taking place cleared up any doubts.

"Please tell me this is not happening?"

Even though it was obvious Kip intended to pitch her voice low enough for only Cameron to hear, Max's rumble of laughter let them know he'd heard her loud and clear. Cameron tried not to snort at the horror in her voice. In spite of her obvious shock over their current location, he was damn proud of her, especially since he was still considering running for the hills. He didn't need to speak to or see any of these people ever again, except he sort of did.

Given the shit direction his mood

had taken since Kip had kicked him out of her bedroom the night before, Cameron very much feared she was indeed necessary to his existence. The realization did nothing to help his current mood. Without warning, Max drew up short. The narrow hallway, combined with walking on each other's heels, had Kip colliding with his back. Chills raced down his body. His skin tightened. She didn't back away. Instead, her hands found Cameron's waist, making him realize her actions had been intentional.

Kip's hitched breath vibrated against his back. A moan rose in his throat. His cock lengthened. Unable to stop from doing so, Cameron dropped his chin to his chest. As his gaze collided with the hands encircling his waist, Cameron realized there'd never been any chance he was leaving here without having her. He couldn't look away.

"It'll be a minute. They're opening up another private room for us."

Max's announcement shook Cameron from his haze enough to allow him to lift his head. His gaze clashed with Ryan's. For once, the man wasn't smiling. Something about this place had changed him, turning Ryan deadly serious. In his confusion, Cameron glanced at Max. His focus was locked on Ryan. The open hunger on Max's face left Cameron speechless. The three of them had served together in Afghanistan. He'd known them for years...since before his scars and nightmares. He'd seen them at their worst. They'd seen him at his lowest. Those years didn't mean shit. He was staring at strangers. Cameron realized something monumental. It was almost big enough to rock him from his lust. He didn't know the pair at all. In this place, they were real. Raw.

"Please follow me?"

Even as their host appeared at Ryan's side, ready to lead them into their own space, Ryan still didn't look away from Cameron. Holding Cameron's stare, Ryan reached for Max. With Max's t-shirt clutched between his fingers, Ryan hauled the man against his chest. His light-green gaze held Cameron transfixed. As Ryan lowered his chin, touching his lips to Max's, Ryan still refused to break eye contact.

Behind the zipper of his jeans, Cameron's dick begged for attention. As if Kip read his thoughts, her hands slid lower. She moved slowly, torturing him. His muscles rippled, bunching in anticipation of each new inch of skin she caressed. Ryan's lids fell closed. He stepped backward, hauling Max along with him without breaking their kiss.

Without Ryan's eyes holding Cameron transfixed, he shook off the trance and moved out of Kip's arms. She let him go. Max and Ryan followed the club's guide without as much as separating an inch. If anything, they seemed to move closer to each other. Cameron took great pains to avoid making eye contact with anyone.

"Cozy," Kip said, laughter lacing her voice as the room came into view.

\*

A circular and padded, knee-high table with several pockets on the side sat in the center of the room. It reminded Kip of the back of an airline seat for some reason. Maybe because she had the same overwhelming desire to check out the contents of each pocket. The moment they were gathered around it, Kip gave in to temptation. With the tip of her fingernail, she pulled open one of the pockets and peeked inside.

The first pouch contained several foil-packaged condoms. In the next she found sample-size and multi-flavored lubricants.

"I wouldn't have pegged you for a germaphobe," Ryan said, startling Kip.

She'd been taking great pains to avoid looking in his direction. If there was a time she'd been more uncomfortable, she couldn't remember it, and she'd been arrested before. Her gaze shot to his. His eyes shone with laughter.

"You're fingering that as if you expect something will jump out and attack."

Taking his words as a challenge, Kip shoved her hand inside, digging around until she found a cherry-flavored sample. She held it up. "My favorite."

"Awesome," Ryan said, cheerfully snagging the packet from her and tearing it open. "I love cherries too."

Funny. She didn't think they were talking about the same thing. He'd become someone she didn't know. A devilish light entered his eyes as he squeezed a drop onto his finger. Before she had time to guess at his intentions, Ryan leaned over and swiped it across her bottom lip. Once he was there, touching her mouth, Kip found she couldn't move away. He stroked her lip again, as if weaving a trance. There was a voice in the back of her mind telling her this was wrong. She ignored it. There was another one wanting to crack a joke about him using it wrong. Lube lip-gloss wasn't her thing. It seemed when Ryan was the one applying it she was on board.

Her shock doubled when he swept in and opened his mouth over her bottom lip.

He hummed against her mouth. Her sex quivered at the sound.

"Delicious," he said before lightly brushing his tongue along hers and then retreating. "Don't be good, Kip. Be good at it."

Twisting around, he dove for Max, consuming him and leaving her on fire.

Kip wanted to tear her gaze away from the pair. She was incapable. They were beautiful together. Women flooded to their self-defense class, no doubt fantasizing about just this type of moment. Nothing she could've possibly conjured compared to the real thing. Max and Ryan were intense and erotic. They were focused and controlled. Her pussy clenched with desire. It didn't matter she would never get to participate. Their lust was tangible. It thickened the air, caressing her skin. The phantom sensation was so real it took a moment for her to realize Cameron's knuckles were grazing her arm. She glanced his way. His expression bordered on predatory. Her tongue shot out, moistening her lips in anticipation of his kiss. Cherry coated her taste buds.

"You look neglected."

At his quietly spoken claim, Kip's gaze dropped to his mouth. There was hunger and then there was what she felt for him. It was almost painful. Of all the ideas she'd formed about Cameron's personality, being in this place wasn't one. He wouldn't make the first move, of that Kip was sure. Reaching over, she snagged the front of his t-shirt. He came willingly when she tugged him toward her. As their mouths collided, he led her free hand toward his jeans. She shaped his erection through the material as her tongue twined with his. The man was beyond delicious.

Cameron was the first to break. She knew he would be. He was barely contained lava disguised as a man. Her scalp stung as he snagged the back of her head and took control of their kiss. Kip tilted her chin back, surrendering. He set the pace as his tongue curled around hers. A stuttered breath came from the back of his throat, vibrating through their kiss. She moaned at the sensation. Kip's panties dampened to the point of being uncomfortable. She wanted them gone. Fingers caressed her cheek. She was almost certain they weren't Cameron's. She didn't give a fuck.

Cameron nipped at her lips. "I'm going to fuck you. If you have a problem with that, now is the time to speak up."

She didn't. Cameron came out of his shirt before coming back for more tongue action. It took every ounce of Kip's willpower not to reach between her legs and relieve some of the pressure building there. Her clit was pulsing and begging. It wouldn't wait forever. The unmistakable sound of belts coming off filled the air, competing against Ryan's moans.

For a moment, Ryan won. Kip needed to see his face. She turned her head and Cameron's lips moved to her throat. The flush of arousal on Ryan's cheeks made his green eyes shine brighter than usual. He stared back even as Max took him from behind. Kip's mouth went dry. Tomorrow, she wouldn't be able to look him in the eye. Tonight, she couldn't tear her eyes away. He was more than gorgeous.

Cameron forced her back on track.

The vision of him rolling on a condom held her captivated. She'd been so fascinated by Ryan and Max she hadn't heard Cameron opening it. Her brain had retreated into some form of horny, dreamlike state where nothing felt real. As the cool air brushed her ass, Kip recognized how real things were. Cameron had somehow divested her of her clothes while she'd been stuck in a lust-filled haze. She would have Cameron while Ryan and Max watched. The real Kip—the one she'd kept hidden for too long—came to the surface. She'd been sleepwalking through life.

Cameron urged her forward until she was leaning on the table for support. The blood rushing through her ears drowned out all sound. Cameron's fingers tightened on her hips as his cock probed at her wet pussy lips. Her walls stretched wide to accommodate Cameron's girth. She couldn't contain her gasp when he finally surged forward, impaling her. She'd wanted him for too long. It was better than her dreams.

With Cameron's hand splayed wide between her breasts, he urged her back against his chest. Her heart slammed against his palm. It was as if it understood its place and fought to meet its owner. His teeth scraped her lobe. Hot breath brushed the column of her throat, causing her nipples to harden almost painfully. With his dick filling her and holding her in place, Cameron spoke against her ear, keeping his voice low and for her alone.

"I ache for you. Goddamn, Kip. I don't want to fight anymore."

Her soul screamed. The shock that had kept her mind fogged lifted, burned away by his ragged words. Kip's heart whimpered. Even as fingers of electricity moved through her, exploding into a blinding light and making her convulse with pleasure, she knew. They'd been fighting fate. Cameron massaged her breasts. His teeth sank into her shoulder. Something inside her shifted as he moaned against her nape because fuck what people say. It was so much worse to love and lose than to never know love at all, and lose she would. This overwhelming sensation in the center of her chest couldn't be denied and she recognized what she'd been struggling against. When it came to her life or anything to do with her heart, Kip ended up wrecked every fucking time.

# Chapter Three

Sensual destruction. That's what Kip meant to Cameron's life. One day, he'd been content in his more-secret-than-not longing for Kip. The next, Cameron spent every second counting the minutes until he could be with her again. Chill bumps rose on his skin and his stomach muscles tightened as the memory of Kip's kiss flared to life. The way she'd hummed from the back of her throat as Cameron sank into her was as clear in his mind now as the moment it happened.

Twice he pulled out his phone, intent on calling Kip. Both times, he put it away without pressing a single number. Ryan and Max had surprised them. Neither Kip nor Cameron had been willing to back out but what if their night together was a slice out of time, never meant for duplication? Chances were good Kip would be embarrassed to see him again. In fact, their parting the night before had been awkward and stilted. He was such a dumbass. Kip was his friend. Yeah...he was carrying around an ass-ton of hidden feelings for her, but he didn't want to lose the friendship part. It was important to him.

With no real thought of doing so, Cameron found himself parked behind G. Richards Bookstore where Kip worked. He knew she was inside. She always worked from noon to six p.m. on Sundays. Throwing open his car door, Cameron blew out a sigh. He even knew her fucking work schedule, for Christ's sake. This whole situation was hopeless.

To his surprise, as he entered, Kip's face lit at the sight of him. She was so freaking beautiful. Her red hair fell over one shoulder, begging him to touch it. Cameron knew how soft it was and his palms itched. Her shell-pink lips tasted like cherries, even without Ryan's help. It was probably some sort of lip-gloss but fuck if he cared. The flavor was seared into his brain.

"I was just dialing your number," she said, flashing her phone at him.

"Really?" Yep...he sounded like a lovesick loser and he didn't give a damn.

As he reached the edge of the counter, she set the phone aside and reached for him.

"I wanted to hear your voice caressing my ear."

Her confession lit him up from the inside. With her finger looped between the buttons on his shirt, Kip tugged him forward. She dragged out his anticipation by moving slowly and giving him time to reject her. Kip didn't turn away. She was happy to see him. That was the sort of thing that could make a man into an addict.

A tiny smile hovered on Kip's lips and a wicked glint shone in her eyes. The world disappeared around him as his mouth collided with hers. With his palms braced against the edge of the counter, Cameron didn't touch her in any other way. It didn't matter. As Kip opened her mouth over his bottom lip, he felt more connected to her than ever before. Her tongue toyed with the crease in his lip. His heart beat a rapid pattern against the wall of his chest. Even if Cameron jogged five miles, he couldn't get his heart rate as high as it was now. The scent of honeysuckle filled his nostrils. He didn't know if it was the air or her skin but he knew he'd never encounter the fragrance again without remembering this moment.

As his lips parted, accepting her tongue, he recognized the way he felt about her wasn't something that would go away. He'd never stood a chance. Their tongues brushed briefly before Kip pulled away but she didn't release her hold on his shirt.

"I think about your mouth all the time," she said, sounding breathless. "You don't kiss me often enough."

A smile burst from Cameron's heart and exploded across his face. He was incapable of stopping it. A loud and irritated sigh tore through the air behind him.

"For the love of all things holy, can I please just get a fucking cup of coffee? Some of us have real jobs to get to."

Kip didn't break eye contact nor did she seem the least bit concerned about the asshole waiting in line behind Cameron. The guy snapped his fingers.

Cameron hated that shit. "He realizes I'm carrying a gun, right?"

With a chuckle, Kip released him. "It's hot as hell too but don't worry, you won't need to shoot him. I'll spit in his drink."

In spite of her smile, Cameron got the feeling she wasn't joking. Glancing around, he spotted Kurt's wife, McKenna, seated nearby. As the owner of G. Richards, she didn't seem the least bit concerned by the drama, but still. Cameron didn't want Kip to lose her job. She had a child to support.

"I'll go distract your boss while you do."

McKenna was the most addictive person Cameron had ever met. She'd captured the heart of every fighter on the

MMA circuit with her odd nature and wit. If she wasn't married to one of the deadliest men on the planet, Cameron imagined the men would be lined up around the building right now. They practically were anyhow. Even the men who didn't play for her team couldn't stay away.

"It's been a while," McKenna said when he reached the edge of her table.

With her head bent over an open notebook and pen in hand, Cameron had no idea how she knew it was him.

"It has," he agreed as he snagged the chair across from her.

Pushing the notebook aside, McKenna met his gaze. The way her eyes latched on to his face, leaving him exposed, reminded Cameron of why people had such a hard time staying away from her. She saw people all the way to their soul.

"Kip should've put some hot sauce in that guy's drink instead of spitting in it. It would've been that much more satisfying."

Cameron blushed. God help him. He didn't even know why nor could he stop it from happening. "Caught all that, did you?"

McKenna's gaze moved over his face. Her expression gave nothing away. "Of course. I notice everything."

For some reason, one Cameron couldn't explain, he felt as if he was in the hot seat. He shifted, uncomfortable. "Hot sauce, huh?" he asked, just to fill his end of the conversation. "Does that mean you're not upset?"

McKenna's shoulder lifted in a half-shrug. "It gave me a chance to steal the guy's newspaper while he was distracted."

A burst of unexpected laughter exploded from Cameron. McKenna was outrageous. Swiping at his eyes, Cameron did his best to contain his humor. "Were there any good stories in there?"

McKenna shrugged again. "How should I know? I don't read the paper."

Cameron shook his head. Talking to McKenna never got old. She ran circles around people with her words, making them work for every foothold. For lack of a better description, she was fun. "You do realize you've just confessed to an officer of the law."

One corner of McKenna's mouth lifted. "I have handcuffs in my purse if you'd like to arrest me."

"If only you were joking."

Besides being the owner of G. Richards, McKenna was a bestselling, hard-core erotica author. She forced people to measure their every word with a naughty scale. She was fiendish as hell. Cameron had known her husband Kurt for a long time and, considering the man's sexual proclivities, Cameron knew McKenna had to be kinky as sin to snag Kurt's attention permanently the way she had. Everyone else suspected it as well. Another mark in her favor.

"Did you have fun last night?" she asked.

The way McKenna held his gaze made him wonder if she was trying not to look in Kip's direction. He did his best to keep from smiling like an idiot. "It was great."

McKenna switched her gaze to her notebook, scribbling something. "You didn't let Max and Ryan talk you into going with them to that underground sex club, did you?"

It was as if the planets were aligned against him. Tossing a quick glance around the room, hoping to avoid her question, Cameron caught sight of Josh lingering in the corner and nursing a coffee. He wasn't looking at Kip but he was there. For the life of him, Cameron couldn't understand why Kip couldn't see how hooked the man was. A smirk pulled at the corners of Cameron's mouth. Kip had spent the night with Cameron. Josh was wasting his time. Something wicked rose up inside Cameron.

"Yes. That's exactly what we did."

McKenna snorted before covering her mouth to silence it. Her eyes shone with mirth as she physically tried to hold in her laughter. After a few deep breaths, she cleared her throat. "Good for you."

"Yep. Lucky me."

The devious grin touching

McKenna's lips would've put the devil's to shame. "Lucky Kip."

*

Cameron's dark-blue police uniform shouldn't have been so fucking sexy but it was. Something about him toting a gun kicked up his hotness level by ten degrees. The things she could do with the handcuffs at his side. The thought alone had Kip pressing her thighs together. Damn. The things he did to her heart. Maybe if she hadn't wanted him for so long, he wouldn't have this effect on her, but the truth was there, staring her in the face.

One day soon, Cameron would hate her. All her secrets—her past—it would all bubble to the surface the way shit always did. He would look at her differently. Kip cut those thoughts off before they could destroy her.

Cameron laughed at something McKenna said. The sound cut through her depressing thoughts, caressing her skin and hardening her nipples. Feeling magnanimous, Kip handed the douche his coffee—free of charge and spit. Appearing somewhat mollified, he stepped aside, allowing Kip the freedom to watch Cameron unimpeded. He was a warrior. That was what she pictured every time she heard his name. The things he'd sacrificed for his country amazed her. A fresh wave of depression washed over her. This man was a patriot. Most would consider her a traitor. If she was a better a person, she'd let him go before she ruined him.

As she looked on, McKenna said something that caused Cameron to turn in his seat and meet Kip's gaze. Kip didn't know why, but heat flooded her cheeks. The expression Cameron wore said it all.

She didn't need to hear what they were discussing. Cameron stood, and without breaking eye contact, he moved across the room. Kip couldn't look away. Weak. She was weak and they could've been alone for all the attention he paid the surrounding people. This time of day was always busy. People slammed G. Richards, hunting their second wave of coffee, hoping to make it through the rest of their work schedule. Cameron ignored them all. This was why she couldn't stay away. He always watched her as if no one else existed. Sex had made him twice as intense. She was hooked.

"If only you could see the way you're looking at me right now," Cameron said the moment he reached her.

"Funny. I was just thinking the same thing about you." Kip heard the breathless note to her voice. She didn't give a damn.

A ghost of a smile passed over his lips. "Would you and Jade like to spend some time with me tonight?"

Kip's throat tightened. He was so perfect. Most men wouldn't have wanted to include her daughter but Cameron would never be most men.

"I'd love that." Damn it. She really would.

* * * * *

When Cameron arrived at Terry and Brian's house, it was lit up like Mardi Gras. There weren't any extra cars in the driveway but the place was obviously occupied. There was a note taped to the back door with a single word written on it. "Basement." Cameron let himself in. He could hear the rhythmic punches and laughter coming from Terry's gym before Cameron even made it to the stairs.

The bright yellow and stainless steel kitchen gleamed, making Cameron wonder if Terry and Brian had a maid. He'd never seen one there, but with their money, they could afford to hire an entire staff. When he reached the doorway leading down into the basement, the laughter increased and Terry's deep rumble floated up the staircase. Cameron's steps slowed even as his heart sped. It was ridiculous the way he wanted to swipe his palms down his jeans to calm the nerves jumping in his stomach. He'd known Kip a long time. There was no logical explanation for his sudden onset of nerves but there it was. He hadn't felt this alive in a decade and the person responsible was steps away. Cameron didn't know if he could force his feet to move. Terry's face appeared at the bottom of the steps.

"Come on. Jade's showing us her moves."

Kip peeked around the corner as well. The smile on her face stole his breath. "Hey, baby," she said.

Like that, Cameron was set free. He had to stop himself from taking the stairs two at a time to reach her faster. The show going on in the basement was the perfect example of grown men wrapped around a little girl's finger. Brian was on his stomach, pretending Jade had him pinned to the mat. Even though Jade was still too small to understand anything to do with MMA, it hadn't stopped the men from involving her in everything, including their training. Cameron couldn't count the number of times Kip had been forced to stop them from trying to wrap Jade's knuckles.

Jade crawled over Brian's back,

using the man as her personal play gym. Her blonde curls stuck out in every direction and to her face, proving how hard she'd been at it. A set of blue eyes peeked over Brian's side, spotting Cameron. She pointed at him.

"Cam!"

The smile tugging at Cameron's lips was beyond his control. He loved the little monster. He pointed back. "Princess!"

She hid her face. "No."

Cameron chuckled over the denial. She was the only little girl he'd ever met who hated princesses. "What are you today then?"

She crawled on her hands and knees, barking.

"Yep. That's my little angel, the dog," Kip informed him as she towed him in for a kiss.

His heart soared. No one batted an

eye. It had always been them even if they took forever to get it together. At first, they'd had a kinship Cameron couldn't explain. Most people overlooked him. Kip never had. The idea of this woman belonging to him was addicting. By the time they werc a few months into their newly found friendship, Cameron had realized no one but her would ever be enough for him.

Brian pushed to his feet. "Don't burn down the house while we're gone."

His announcement caught Cameron's attention. "Don't run off on my account."

"Nah," Brian said, waving off Cameron's words. "We're not. McKenna invited us over. It's time we spread the love and spoil the niece."

Terry swooped in and stole Jade's kisses, making her squeal.

"Yeah," Terry agreed, as he set Jade on her feet. "We're not content to ruin just one child. It's our life's purpose to make these little girls unbearable for the men of the future."

Cameron wanted to believe Terry was joking, but even if he was, it was still true. Jade and Tayrn would be hell on wheels one day.

"We can take Jade with us if the two of you want to go do something."

Cameron scoffed at Terry's offer as he swept Jade from the floor. "No way. You've had her all day. Let someone else have a turn. We're just going to hang out and watch a movie unless Jade wants to do something else." He looked at the little girl in his arms and his eyebrows rose in question.

"Fight," Jade demanded, much to Brian and Terry's delight.

Their laughter followed them all the way up the stairs. Cameron shook his head. She was such a mess.

Brian reversed course. "Speaking of fights... Kip has one Friday night. I'm going in as her cornerman. You going to go and keep Terry out of trouble while we're busy?"

"As if I ever cause trouble," Terry called from the top of the stairs.

Cameron couldn't stop smiling. Their house was such a happy home. It was impossible not to get sucked into that zone.

"Sure. I'll be there."

"Cool."

With a nod, Brian disappeared, leaving Cameron alone with his two favorite girls. He was ready to make the most of their time together.

\* \* \* \* \*

The light from the TV flickered off Cameron's face, fascinating Kip. Cameron lay sprawled across the couch with Jade on his chest. The pair slept peacefully through the entire movie. Kip couldn't take her eyes off them. They looked so content. She hated to break it up but Jade needed to be in bed. As gently as possible, Kip eased Jade from Cameron's hold. Her eyes peeked open a few times on the way to her room but she was out cold by the time Kip tucked her into bed.

The bigger of Kip's two sleeping beauties was another matter. She wanted to tuck him into bed as well, but she needed him awake. Three steps outside Jade's bedroom, a solid weight surrounded her, catching her off guard. Cameron's mouth covered hers, swallowing her surprised gasp. Everything about Cameron appealed to her. His scent.

The way his skin felt beneath her fingers. No one else made her feel since her heart had frozen. When Cameron was around, she felt too much.

Kip willingly accepted his consumption. Cameron's teeth nipped at her lips. His tongue sought hers. Her body hummed. The tips of Cameron's fingers skimmed her sides as he tugged her shirt up even as he urged her toward her room. Chill bumps rose on her skin behind the trail of his fingers. Kip leaned away long enough for Cameron to work the shirt over her head and toss it onto the floor before she went back for more.

"Your mouth is amazing," Kip said against his lips, before swiping his tongue with hers. "Every time I see you, I want to taste it." She sank her teeth into his bottom lip to prove her point even as she reached for the button of his jeans. "But that's not the only part of you I want to lick."

Kip slipped to her knees. She couldn't see a thing in the pitch-dark bedroom but she didn't need a light for this. The instant she set Cameron's erection free, she wrapped her lips around his crown. Sucking in an audible breath, Cameron brushed her hair aside before cupping the back of her head. His hand immediately fell away as if he feared she would stop if he turned demanding.

"I won't break," she promised before taking him down her throat.

The sound Cameron made as she swallowed him made her heart soar, spurring her on. Hollowing her cheeks, she let him slip almost all the way from her mouth before letting him back in. His fingers found her hair once more. This time, her scalp stung as his grip tightened.

She toyed with his slit before circling his crown and teasing the sensitive nerve ending in a move she knew would drive him insane. His hips rolled and she knew she'd won.

"Goddamn, Kip."

His guttural voice went straight to her already soaking-wet pussy, making it pulse. He always set her on fire with barely a heated glance. Having the man this hot and in her mouth made her squirm with longing. She stroked the length of him as she begged for him to give her everything.

"Fuck my mouth, Cameron. I want it." Tomorrow, she'd feel the sting of mortification. Tonight, she wanted Cameron's salty cum filling her mouth and to know she was the reason.

Taking her at her word, Cameron pumped against her mouth. Kip took everything he gave. Her fingernails sank into the backs of Cameron's thighs, hoping to get a quarter of an inch closer to him.

"Fuck. Jesus. Oh my God."

His words didn't make sense past that point, exactly as Kip intended. A hoarse cry left his throat as his orgasm hit. Kip swallowed the creamy liquid, failing to get it all. It was a mess and she didn't care. In that moment, Kip owned him and she belonged to him. For a minute out of time, she could forget the other voices in her head, reminding her of the truth she couldn't speak. He owned a lie.

# Chapter Four

Cameron caught a flash of blue out of the corner of his eye, causing him to turn. He wished like hell he could've been surprised to see Josh among the crush at Warehouse District but somehow he'd known the man would turn up. There was every probability Josh was scheduled to fight tonight in one of the brutal, no-holds-barred bouts Warehouse was known for. Like several of the men Cameron knew, Josh took part almost every weekend. There was a hell of a lot of money in unsanctioned bouts...if you survived the lifestyle long enough. In his heart, Cameron knew Josh wasn't here to fight. Josh was there for Kip. It didn't matter what Kip claimed, Cameron saw the situation from a man's point of view. There was no way Josh had given up nor would he leave her alone. As a matter of point, Cameron wondered how many encounters she'd had with the man since her last fight. It wasn't likely Kip would tell him after the way he'd reacted the last time Josh had shown up here.

Kip appeared at the mouth of the cage, preparing for inspection before entering the octagon. Brian stood proudly at her side, going in as her cornerman. As predicted, Josh's attention fixed upon her and didn't move. Even from Cameron's vantage point, he didn't miss the predatory gleam in the other man's eyes. Shit. Eventually this would implode.

Shooting a quick glance in Terry's direction, Cameron noticed Terry too had spotted Josh in the crowd. Cameron almost took a step back at Terry's expression. Cameron was staring at a stranger—a hardened and deadly version of the Terry who'd been standing beside him only moments earlier. Cameron didn't know how else to explain the change that had overcome the man. His face was carved of steel but his eyes were maniacal. They promised death.

"I take it you haven't seen Josh since his argument with Kip."

Terry's gaze flickered in Cam's direction for a second. "Nope. I knew I'd find him eventually."

Josh turned his head. As if he felt Terry's stare, Josh focused on the man. His expression matched Terry's, openly challenging him to make a move. Cameron was switching his gaze between the pair, incapable of doing anything else. Terry smirked. It was terrifying. There was nothing left of the man Cameron knew. Josh turned and pushed his way toward the door. It was obvious to anyone watching he expected Terry to follow. Terry cast a quick glance in Cameron's direction.

"I'll be back."

He was gone before Cameron could protest. The bell rang and Kip's name filled the air, pulling Cameron's attention toward the octagon. He was torn. This night was about Kip but there was a voice inside his head, screaming for him to follow Terry. He took a step in that direction. The sound of flesh meeting flesh and the howl of the crowd had Cameron's focus returning to the match. A mob of people swarmed closer to the cage, making it impossible for Cameron to move.

To keep from picturing the thousand horrors Terry was—most likely—raining down upon Josh's head, Cameron tried to concentrate on Kip's every move. She lasted a full round without getting hit in the face, which was her biggest weakness. Terry had been working on her style, helping her improve on protecting her head, but Kip was still new to the sport. She had a ways to go. It would take time.

Kip landed a solid kick to her opponent's ribs before executing a perfect sweep. The other woman went down but sprang back up immediately, unaffected. At this rate, they could go all night. Was Terry okay? Cameron shook his head. He couldn't let himself go there. The man was more than capable of taking care of himself. *Yeah but is he stuffing Josh's body in a dumpster?* Fuck. Kip won and Cameron had missed it. With her arms raised in victory, Kip met his stare. The luminous smile stretching her lips stole every ounce of his concern for Terry. Cameron loved it when she was happy.

119

She'd searched for his face in her moment of triumph. The realization did something to his chest.

"She looks happy."

Cameron's heart jumped into his throat when Terry spoke close to Cameron's ear. Glancing over his shoulder, he searched Terry's features for any signs he'd confronted Josh. There was nothing. Not a single mark marred his skin. It was scary how relaxed he seemed when only minutes earlier he'd looked ready to slaughter the other man.

"She does," Cameron agreed. "Did you kill him?"

A hint of a smile hovered on Terry's lips. He didn't respond nor would he meet Cameron's stare.

"We should go save Kip before she's mobbed by this rowdy bunch," Terry said, letting Cameron know the topic was closed.

Since it was obvious Terry had no intention of discussing what went down with Josh, Cameron headed for the pathway between the cage and locker rooms, hoping to reach Kip before she was carried away by the tidal wave of people swarming her.

"I won," Kip cheered when she caught sight of them.

Terry said his congrats before turning his attention Brian's way. Kip threw herself at Cameron. His arms encircled her body, squeezing her to his chest without a single qualm. Even when his mind was too slow to keep up with her, his body knew where she belonged.

"I won," Kip repeated, sounding amazed.

"I'm so proud of you, baby." He wanted her to have the world. "How should we celebrate?"

Kip took a step back, pulling a face. "Right now, I need a shower. Sorry. Now you're covered in my sweat."

The evil grin popped into place before Cameron could think twice. "I love being covered in your sweat." He cast a glance in Terry's direction, ensuring the men were still occupied with each other. "McKenna has Jade all night. There's a shower at my place."

Her gaze swept his body, leaving him heated everywhere it touched. "So there is. I have to grab my bag."

"Make it quick." For real, he didn't know how long he could wait to be alone with her.

* * * * *

Even though Kip had been to Cameron's house several times, she'd never stayed the night. First off, she'd never had a reason, but also there was Jade to consider. Tonight, Kip had the man all to herself. She was giddy. That was a word she'd never considered using when referring to herself, but there it was. Kip couldn't deny the way her excitement ran through her in waves. As his three-bedroom, tan brick home came into view, the sensation grew until Kip swore she was seconds away from levitating in her seat. A bit of adrenaline still might be keeping her high but Kip couldn't deny Cameron was the cause of her excitement.

He was a warrior. Maybe people would think she was being poetic or some shit by thinking of him that way. She'd never cared what people thought. That was the word that ran through her mind every time she looked at him. He was scarred and hardened by battle. She wanted to touch him and own him. Every time she did, Kip felt powerful. In her lifetime, she'd felt helpless more times than not. Being with Cameron was a heady thing.

As they made their way to the front door, Kip followed his lead since he had the keys. It also gave her an excuse to watch his ass. Curling her hands into fists, Kip barely resisted the urge to squeeze his cheeks. Fuck it. She cupped his ass. Some temptations weren't meant to be denied. This was one. He glanced over his shoulder. The way his cheek curved into a smile let her know he wasn't annoyed. Good. She didn't relent.

"You're so fucking sexy."

His low chuckle at her claim washed over her, dampening her panties. "I'm serious, Cameron. You're killing me."

He fumbled with the keys in the lock. Her arms encircled his waist. As part of Terry's soldier rehabilitation program, Cameron worked out and sparred hard almost every day. It showed. The ridges of his abs drew her fingertips toward them because that's what yummy abs did. They whispered for women to feel of them. Who was she to deny them? Each line she traced caused her pussy to pulse with need. Kip was damn near dancing in place by the time Cameron opened the door.

A blast of cold air washed over her. It did nothing to cool her skin. Heat radiated from her body. It was dark inside except for a soft light coming from inside the kitchen.

It cast a slight glow over the living room, illuminating their path enough so they didn't run into any furniture. His home was all man, just like he was. Big TV, leather furniture and sturdy oak tables filled the living room. She knew from previous visits that every appliance he owned was stainless steel. It was also military clean. He'd told her once that some habits were hard to break. It was a habit they didn't share.

Cameron led her past the bathroom in the hall, heading for his room. "No one ever uses that shower so there're no toiletries in there."

Kip didn't care where they went as long as she could get him inside her as quickly as possible. She ached. "All right."

As they cleared the bedroom door, Kip tucked her fingers into his back pocket to keep from running into anything. It was too dark for her to make out a thing. When he flipped on the bathroom light, she considered hissing like a vampire. Tiny bursts of what looked like lightning popped behind her closed lids from the sudden change.

"Sorry. I should've given you a little warning."

Kip blinked against the assault. "It's okay. I'm good."

The tiny bathroom finally came into focus and she tried taking a step inside. Cameron drew her up short. He looked unsure of himself.

"I guess it's a lot smaller than you're used to."

A snort escaped before she could think better of it. Sometimes she forgot that Cameron knew nothing about the real her. One day, she'd have to tell him everything, but not today. Since telling him the bathroom was bigger than anything she'd grown up with would open a conversation she didn't want to start, Kip chose a different tactic. "It's perfect. There's less room for you to get away."

With a roll of his eyes, Cameron

backed out of her way. "I'll leave you to it. There're towels in the closet behind the door."

A sigh of disappointment ran through her. She'd been looking forward to watching beads of water run down his body while steam surrounded them. It seemed he didn't feel the same.

"Okay." Even if she'd tried, Kip couldn't have kept the disappointment from her voice.

Cameron's brows drew together as if he was attempting to decipher her tone. She didn't care how she sounded. There wasn't a doubt in her mind it was his head that was keeping him away. She hadn't missed the way he'd carefully avoided her seeing too much of him unclothed. The night they'd shared a private room with Max and Ryan, he'd taken her from behind. That night had been delicious.

She'd thought little of his purposeful positioning at the time. The second time they were together, the room had been dark and Cameron was gone before morning. Whether Cameron admitted it or not she knew him.

This so wasn't happening on her watch. "Oh. Damn. I forgot my bag in the car." Cameron's expression cleared. "I'll go grab it."

The second he disappeared, Kip set to work. In a matter of seconds, she had the water at the perfect temperature and was stripped down to nothing. Cameron rounded the corner, bag in hand, and froze. A wave of heat blasted her. The lust radiating from his eyes held her captive. His gaze raked her body. The muscles in her stomach clenched as the muscle in his jaw ticked. He didn't move. Kip's lungs burned, making her realize she was holding her breath.

"Come here."

At her demand, Cameron set aside the bag before dutifully doing as she asked. He stood toe-to-toe with her, staring down at her with open hunger.

"Take off your clothes."

He glanced away, not meeting her gaze. "I'm waiting, Cameron."

When he didn't move fast enough, Kip reached for the hem of his shirt. This was happening. He would let her in. To Kip's surprise, he didn't stop her as she eased the material upward. The closed expression he wore stabbed her through the heart. He expected the worst. It would never happen. Once the shirt was high enough to expose his stomach and chest, Kip inspected every inch. There were angry red scars—she'd been expecting them—but they weren't what she really saw. It was his lead-a-girl-to-hell abs along with the deep valley at the center of his chest that captured her gaze.

She closed the final inch between them and opened her mouth over his chest. Damn. It tasted every bit as delicious as it looked. A hum rose in her throat. The shirt disappeared. If his skin hadn't been delighting her taste buds, it might've surprised her he'd willingly tossed the garment aside. All she knew at the moment was desire. She reached for the button on his jeans, working it loose before sliding down his zipper. As she pushed the material down his hips, Kip couldn't look away. His body was amazing.

Cameron touched her chin, tilting back her head and forcing her to meet his stare. His eyes searched her face as if he couldn't decide if her reactions were genuine. There was no way she could hide her body's response to him. He was killing her. Kip's clit pulsed, begging for his touch. Water filled her mouth at the thought of straddling his sexy hips and having his controlled power between her thighs. Snagging his hand, she slid it down her body, moving slowly and torturing them both. Her eyes threatened to fall closed as his palm scraped over her sensitized nipple but she forced them to stay focused on his face. When she reached the apex of her thighs, Cameron didn't need any further encouragement. The tips of his fingers skimmed her mound. With the lightest pressure, her pussy lips parted beneath his touch. Sparks of electricity ran through her. Pleasure coiled in her stomach. Every muscle in Kip's body tightened with anticipation. By the time Cameron dipped inside her channel, she thought she might scream.

"Damn, Kip. You're so wet."

Kip could barely speak past the lust choking her. "I can't help it. Your body is amazing. I want to do bad things to it."

The final word barely passed her lips before Cameron claimed her mouth. He took a step forward, deepening their kiss while maneuvering her toward the shower. Kip shoved at his jeans, hoping to pry them off, but Cameron didn't stop. With one arm wrapped around her waist, he held her against him as he stepped into the shower, jeans and all. Laughter bubbled in her throat.

"You'll never be able to get those jeans off now."

Cameron dipped his head, drawing her nipple between his teeth. The sensation went straight to her cunt.

"I'm scared of myself right now,"

Cameron said against her skin. "These pants are all that's keeping you safe."

The deep rumble in his voice made her quiver with anticipation. He dropped to his knees.

"In my mind I'm already fucking you and it has nothing to do with pleasure," he added.

Tugging her hips forward, he coaxed her leg over his shoulder. Kip clung to the wall as hot water streamed down her body. She couldn't look away from his face. His expression was feral. Holding her stare, he slowly leaned in.

"It's just me, claiming your body and trying to bury myself so deep inside you, you'll never escape."

His hot mouth covered her pussy, and Kip's knees buckled and she almost went down. Only his grip on her ass and the shoulder supporting her leg kept it from happening. Cameron didn't show an ounce of mercy. His tongue, lips and teeth scraped, tugged and sucked, making her half insane. Her cries echoed from the walls of the tiny shower, filling her ears until the roar of her blood pounding drowned out all sound. All she could do was feel. She ground herself against his mouth, uncaring of anything other than capturing the blinding orgasm Cameron promised. Her muscles tightened around his tongue, attempting to hold him there. It slipped away, tracing a line to her clit, circling and tormenting her. The tips of his fingers skimmed her crack, dipping inside. The coil wound tight inside her snapped. Cameron's name tore from her throat as her vision darkened around the edges. She couldn't draw enough oxygen into her lungs to support her brain. Pulses of pleasure beat between her legs and still

Cameron didn't relent. He growled against her pussy, making her head spin. When Kip thought she couldn't take another second, Cameron shot to his feet, unbalancing her and tossing her over his shoulder. In a fog-like haze, Kip stroked his ass as he headed for the bed.

"You're mine," Cameron said, sounding demonic as he tossed her onto the mattress.

Fuck yeah, she was. Too bad she'd lost the ability to speak.

\*

Kip didn't respond. He couldn't let that stand. It was possible she couldn't catch her breath. Her chest rose and fell with each strained lungful of air, making his already aching cock scream for attention. Cameron didn't hesitate or consider how Kip would react. Snagging the handcuffs from his side table, he snapped them around one of her wrists. Her gaze moved to her arm as if she couldn't quite grasp what he'd done. If she thought to argue, he didn't give her the chance. He held her stare as he urged her arms above her head. Kip didn't fight it. Anticipation had him perched on the edge of insanity. After weaving the empty cuff through the rungs of his headboard, Cameron snapped it closed around her other wrist.

Straightening away, Cameron swept his gaze over her body as he peeled off his wet jeans. Removing the soaked material from his body wasn't fun but the way his jeans ended up that way made it worthwhile. A flush covered Kip's skin. Her nipples were hard, making his mouth water. Everything about her called to him. She might've been chained but she wasn't helpless. Her hooded eyes were heavy with desire as she waited to see what he would do next. For a moment, she pressed her knees together as if her patience was at end, before she allowed them to fall open, tempting him. His dick strained to be closer to her. Moving slowly, hoping to torment her, Cameron found a condom and ripped open the package. He palmed his cock, savoring the way her eyes followed the motion when he stroked it.

"Cameron."

Damn. The breathless way she said his name tightened his skin. He rolled on the condom.

"I don't think you understand your position, Kip. You're mine." She licked her lips. Oh, she was a tease.

"Maybe so, but you're mine too."

He skimmed her inner thigh with the tips of his fingers. His eyebrows rose. "Maybe?"

The sound of her breath catching

filled the air. Her back arched. "Definitely."

His knee hit the mattress between hers. "That's better."

"You gonna keep me locked up all night?"

Instead of answering, Cameron settled between her thighs and closed his lips around her nipple. She made him want everything and dream the world could be his. Even though his body was screaming for release, he wanted to savor every second. Kip's deep moan combined with the flavor of her pussy still lingering on his tongue, making his dick leak. His balls were already drawn up so tightly there was no way he would last.

"If you only knew how many times I've pictured you exactly like this— incapable of getting away," he said, moving from one breast to the other.

Her thighs tightened on his hips as if attempting to lure him inside.

"I could do anything to you right now. Any special requests?" He was dying. It was worth it.

"Inside me. Now," she panted.

A low chuckle rumbled from his chest, sounding sinister even to him. Sliding his cock along her slit, Cameron relished her every pained moan. Her juices soaked his fingers.

"Oh God. Please?"

He did it again, teasing her clit with his crown. The whimper coming from the back of her throat was his undoing. Surging forward, Cameron gasped for air as her tight heat surrounded him. Everything he felt for her clogged his throat. She meant every fucking thing to him. In that moment, he would've killed for her.

\* \* \* \* \*

Cameron's fingers trailed down Kip's arm before moving back up again. He repeated the motion until Kip was having a hard time holding her eyes open. Every muscle felt wonderfully sore. Between her bout and Cameron's lovemaking, she'd be lucky to crawl out of bed in the morning. In spite of her exhaustion, Kip's mind refused to shut down. Tracing a pattern across Cameron's oblique, she stared into the darkness, soaking up the sound of his heart. If he was the least bit concerned over her draping over his body like a blanket, he didn't say a word. There was something rattling around in his brain though. She could practically feel him stewing.

"Out with it," she ordered when she couldn't take any more.

His low chuckle rumbled against

her cheek. "What makes you think there's something to get out?"

"Because I know you. Something's up."

He lasted exactly five seconds. "I talked to my dad today."

"Ha! Called it. What is the elder North up to these days?"

She felt Cameron shrug. "The usual. Working the ranch, disappointed I haven't been home since I got hurt, and coming this way in a few weeks to trade some horses. He wants to meet up in Cottonwood while he's on this side of the U.S. It's a little over four hours' drive but nothing compared to his haul from Athens. I was hoping you and Jade might want to go with me. She'd get to see the horses."

He sounded so hopeful Kip's heart skipped a beat. God. The things this man did to her soul. It wasn't fair.

"I'd love to go with you, but why don't you ever go home?"

Cameron's weight shifted beneath her, making Kip wonder if he was uncomfortable answering the question. She wasn't taking it back. He was a part of her life. She wanted to know everything about him.

Finally, he shrugged again. "Things are different now. I've changed and he's changed." Cameron paused. "No. I'm the only one who's changed. Obviously, I've changed physically but I also don't see things the way I used to. Every time I go back home, I stay in my old room, and everything looks so foreign to me." An aggravated sigh came from the back of his throat. It was sexy. "It's hard to explain. All my childhood memories are still in my head, but I can't remember being that person—innocent and idealistic. I can see the parts of me I've lost too clearly there." Cameron fell silent for a moment before adding, "Well, that went from asking you to go on a fun road trip to being depressing as hell real quick."

Kip disagreed. She found his admission fascinating. There were times she could see the parts of her that were missing with a blinding clarity as well. It sucked. "It's funny."

"What is?" Cameron asked, sounding genuinely interested.

"I've always seen you as innocent and idealistic."

Cameron's chest shook with barely suppressed laughter. Kip loved the way it felt. "Innocent, huh? Maybe we should go out with Ryan and Max again. I don't think I've done enough to disabuse you of that notion."

Kip thanked any and all deities still listening to her for the darkness hiding her face. It burned with mortification. That night was more than the heat of the moment. It was the heat of a thousand moments with Cameron, built up since the first time he'd kissed her and then left her unsatisfied. Kip pinched his side. "I can barely look the two of them in the eye when I go to self-defense class as it is."

Cameron's laughter grew. The sound made her want to be outrageous. She loved it when he was happy.

"I'm being serious. You have no idea how much Ryan enjoys tormenting me. The other day, he gave me a tube of cherry ChapStick because he said he knows it's my favorite."

Cameron was laughing so hard no sound emerged.

"Then when I didn't get one of their

positions right, Max pointed out he knew for a fact I was more flexible than I was letting on."

Cameron swiped at his eyes. "Oh God. We're so going back one of these days."

Huh. Kip did kind of want to go again.

# Chapter Five

Mountie North—honest to God, that was the man's name—looked so much like Cameron, it was eerie. Older and without the scars of course, but he was Cameron in every other way—height, build, eyes...everything. Kip couldn't look away. She also kind of wanted to hug him. It was impossible to avoid an immediate connection with someone who was the replica of someone she loved. For the hundredth time since they arrived at Cottonwood Stables, Kip forced herself to focus on the horses gathering inside the fence instead of Mr. North's slightly mismatched eyes. It didn't last long.

"Kipley, huh? Are your parents hippies?"

This coming from a guy named Mountie. Kip pasted on her brightest smile. "They could've been I suppose, but that's not how I landed the name. I was named after a tiny town in Texas. In the mid-1800s, in the time of the Old West, it was a haven for outlaws. Here you are, named after the police. How ironic the two of us should meet?"

Mountie had a barrel laugh. She didn't know how else to describe it. It came from the chest in a huge bellow. The sound was contagious. Kip couldn't stop smiling. There was no word in the English language that was strong enough to describe how nervous she'd been about doing this. Parents weren't her strong suit. It wasn't as if she'd had practice, and loving parents wanted to know things. What if he had questions she couldn't or wouldn't answer? This was a huge risk.

"Actually I'm named after Mountie Jacobson, the famous gunslinger. So really, how ironic we should meet?"

A burst of unexpected laughter hit Kip. She didn't know if the man was screwing with her but he was quick. Even though Jade was too young to understand their conversation she was momentarily distracted from the animals. She giggled as if she knew what was going on. The sight only made Kip laugh harder. It had been a long time. That thought was sobering. When she stopped to think about it, Kip couldn't remember the last time she'd felt this light.

Jade tugged on the man's pant leg, wanting to be picked up. He didn't hesitate before scooping her up.

"This little one is adorable."

"Thank you." Kip's pulse beat in her ears, stealing the joy from the day.

He would have questions. Cameron hugged her to his side as if he sensed her panic. Her heart slowed.

Two horses moved closer and Jade squealed as she tried squirming from Mountie's arms. She wasn't scared. Jade had no fear. Jade would get those horses if it was the last thing she did. "Horsey."

"Yep. That's Butter and Bean," Mountie said, obviously content to have another horse enthusiast on board.

Kip assumed Butter was the butter-colored one and Bean was the brown one but she didn't ask.

"You want to pet them? They're both big babies."

"No." Jade's answer belied her actions as she threw herself forward in the man's arms.

"Don't worry," Kip assured him. "She says no to everything. I'm certain she can say yes but I've never heard her do so."

Mountie focused on her. "Are you

scared of horses?"

It had been a long time since she'd been around any large animals but they seemed nice enough. "No sir."

"That's good. Climb over that fence and take this little girl to pet Butter and Bean before she explodes."

The expression Cameron wore said a thousand things. All of them led to him dying over this later. He was enjoying the hell out of her discomfort and it looked as if she was climbing a damn fence. Fan-fucking-tastic. As she pulled herself up the first wooden slat, Cameron's hand found her ass. Kip rolled her eyes and considered accidentally on purpose kicking him in the balls before deciding she liked that part of his anatomy too much. Lucky bastard. It wasn't that Kip didn't love the outdoors, she just happened to love the coconut oil, sand between her toes outdoors—not scaling wooden walls and horse shit between her toes outdoors. Only Jade's excitement spurred Kip on. Her willingness to make an ass of herself also had a little to do with the happiness shining in Cameron's eyes. Maybe. A little.

She landed safely on the other side and Cameron kissed her, making her climb worthwhile, before handing Jade over the fence. Kip popped the squirming toddler on her hip and prayed for strength.

"You better be glad I love you, monster," Kip grumbled, heading for the horses that appeared way larger on this side of safety.

"You want to tell me why you never come home?"

Kip picked up the pace at Mountie's rumbled question. Maybe it was safer on this side of the fence after all.

*

The flash in Kip's eyes before she'd turned away promised he'd pay for this later. For now, Cameron was enjoying the moment. It was rare for Kip ever to look out of place. Even inside a hard-core sex club, she'd held her own. A pair of horses and climbing a fence seemed to be the line in the sand. She'd stepped over it. It would be so much fun taking his punishment for this. Unfortunately, the instant she was safely on the other side, his dad had ambushed him. Cameron swore he could feel Kip's evil grin as she walked away, leaving him to his fate. As usual, his dad didn't wait for him to answer before flying into a lecture.

"I mean, at first we thought you stayed in Vegas because that's where your doctors are and you needed your space after what happened. After a while, we thought maybe you loved your job too much to leave. I guess we sort of hoped that was the case since the only other possibility was you didn't want to see us."

All those things were true, to an extent. "Of course I want to see you. I'm here."

His dad snorted. Cameron scrubbed at his face. He'd learned from experience it wouldn't do him any good to argue. His father was bent on delivering a speech. As usual, it wouldn't get him anywhere, but the man wouldn't be happy until he said his piece. Releasing a heavy sigh, Cameron set his elbows on the fence and settled in. Nothing was ever easy where his dad was concerned. In spite of the situation, a smile touched his lips. Butter nosed Kip's elbow, knocking her off balance. Jade's blonde curls bounced as she turned in her mother's arms and pointed a chastising finger at the horse. Even from where he stood he could hear her admonishing, "No, bad horsey." A low chuckle escaped him.

In his distraction, it took a minute for the silence to penetrate his mind. Glancing over, he found his father watching him. There was no way his dad was finished already. Cameron lifted his eyebrows in question.

After a moment of simply staring at him, his father shook his head. "You haven't heard a word I've said, have you?"

Cameron smiled. Unapologetic. His dad blinked as if noticing something for the first time. With a sigh, his dad mimicked Cameron's pose, leaning on the fence.

"Tell me about this girl then if we're not going to talk about anything else."

Cameron stared at Kip, trying to

think of what to say. Thousands of emotions surged through him. "I love her."

"I can see that much for myself. What I was hoping for was a bit more like where's she from? What are her folks like? Do you plan on marrying her?"

Cameron sighed but his dad didn't relent.

"Come on, Cam. You've got to give me something to take home to your mom. She'll want all the details."

That was true. "I believe she's originally from Texas but from what I understand she spent most of her life traveling the world. She doesn't talk about her parents." Kip really didn't talk about her parents. It was odd. He'd never noticed but he hadn't wanted to talk much about his either.

"Don't think I didn't notice you avoided my last question."

Cameron couldn't lie and say he hadn't pictured coming home to Kip and Jade every night. If anything, he could see it too well. He'd fantasized about that life a thousand times since meeting her. What Cameron couldn't envision was Kip saddled with him for life. She could have anyone. What if she looked around and realized it one day? As much as Cameron would like to believe he'd accepted the scars covering over half his body, there was a small part of his brain that couldn't help but wonder why Kip would waste her time on him. She refused to let him hide from her but still... As if she felt his doubt, Kip turned her head and caught him staring. A slow smile stretched her lips. He'd been waiting for that smile. She winked. He knew she was the one.

"Yeah," Cameron said. "She's not getting away from me."

\* \* \* \* \*

The hum of the engine was the only sound filling the otherwise silent car. The occasional set of headlights flashed over Kip's face and every time it happened, Cameron glanced over to make sure she was still sleeping. Jade had worn her out. Not to mention she'd been on top of her game, charming his dad into smiling nonstop. At one point, she'd even made the old man blush. It was no wonder she was exhausted. Even when Cameron realized he was smiling into the darkness like an insane person, he still couldn't stop. Glancing in the mirror, he checked on Jade. Her blonde curls shimmered despite the dark. She was out. A lump rose in Cameron's throat. Everything he loved the most was here in this car. Sometimes, at the oddest moments, he worried it would all slip away.

The face of Kip's phone lit with an incoming call. She didn't stir. Since Brian and Terry had his number, Cameron didn't wake her. If it was an emergency, they could call him. Another car passed and Cameron glanced over again. The sensation in his chest grew. She did something to him. She always had. That was why he'd fought against her so hard. Kip could crush him in an instant and his dad's questions made Cameron realize something he'd intentionally ignored. He knew next to nothing about her life before she came to Vegas.

He knew her. Her smile and kind heart were as familiar to him as his reflection. Her wicked sense of humor and undying loyalty were things he depended on, but he didn't know what had made her who she was. Kip's past was a mystery. In his defense, he had none. Cameron hadn't realized it until he really thought about it but he'd never met a woman who didn't talk about herself until Kip. More than that, she didn't invite other people to turn the conversation her way. She asked pointed questions or spoke of moments that included everyone present. There was never a time he could remember her saying a single thing that led backward. Cameron was as much to blame as anyone—he hadn't asked. It was no secret Josh had abandoned her in Tennessee while she'd been pregnant with Jade. That was as much as Cameron wanted to know about that situation. The last thing he needed was more reason to hate the man.

Cameron took a deep breath. One man's loss was his gain. Kip's phone lit again, illuminating the console between them. It darkened just as quickly. Text message, he surmised, letting it go. She'd see it when she woke up. Barely two minutes passed before it happened again. With a sigh, Cameron glanced at the face. If something had happened to Brian or Terry, he'd feel like shit for ignoring their messages. Josh's name flashed across the screen. Cameron dropped the phone as if it was made of acid.

She would have to deal with Josh eventually. Cameron didn't want to fight and saying anything about the situation with Josh would lead to an argument. It always did but she really couldn't let this go on forever. Kip needed to put her foot down. Josh needed to get out of her life. It drove Cameron insane every time he thought about it. He checked on his girls again. How could anyone walk away from them?

Before Cameron could stop himself, he pulled to the shoulder of the road and was across the car, capturing Kip's mouth. He could feel a smile shaping her lips against his. When her fingers brushed through his hair and her tongue touched the corner of his mouth, Cameron thought his chest would explode. There was so much inside him, begging to escape, he didn't know where to go with it. He'd quietly loved her for so long. Now that he had her, he wanted to smother her in affection. Instead, Cameron tried pouring his love into his kiss. There was no way she couldn't feel it. Even after he'd pulled back an inch, Cameron couldn't move away. The way Kip's fingers rested on his cheek made him wonder if she felt the same.

"I was dreaming about you," Kip whispered. "You were smiling. Don't ever stop doing that. It would break my heart."

Cameron realized Kip was still more

asleep than awake. Guilt ate at him for disturbing her. Sometimes he thought he might go insane if he couldn't touch her.

"Go back to sleep, baby. You still have about an hour."

She was already asleep before Cameron had his seat belt in place. Between Cameron's racing thoughts and his stupid heart making plans for the future, the final hour went by in a blur. He half expected Jade to be raring to go the second the engine died, but neither Kip nor Jade budged. Jade's tiny snores seemed loud now that the car was quiet. Cameron smothered a chuckle over the sound. For a minute, he simply stared at his girls, wanting to keep them. Surely by now they'd accepted they belonged with him. He'd been there since day one. Taking them home and then going home to an empty house had gotten old a long time ago.

Giving up on his hopes for the future for the night, Cameron turned in his seat. Something captured his attention. A wisp of clothing or a brightly colored shoe? Either way, it looked as if someone was sneaking out of Kip's bedroom window. Reaching between his seat and the door, Cameron retrieved his service weapon and quietly exited the car. Staying low, he kept to the fence line and out of sight. The man wasn't running. He was strolling away from the house as if he had every right to be there. The instant Cameron glimpsed his large frame and profile, he knew. This had to end.

"Hands where I can see them."

Josh froze at the bellowed words, fucking Cameron out of the fight he was itching for. With his back to Cameron, Josh held up his hands, showing his surrender.

"On your knees."

One knee hit the ground, followed slowly by the other. Cameron couldn't believe Josh wasn't trying to talk his way out of this or make a run for it. He calmly accepted his fate.

"Hands behind your head."

As Josh laced his fingers behind his head, Cameron moved in, keeping his service weapon trained to the back of Josh's skull. Cameron wasn't taking any chances. All he needed was an excuse and Josh wouldn't live to see another day. Rage like Cameron had never known flooded his veins. This man was a plague upon the lives of the woman and child Cameron loved. Never again.

"No!"

The scream ripped through the night air, startling him. Kip raced in their direction. Josh shifted forward as if he meant to meet her halfway. Cameron pressed the gun closer.

"Don't move," Cameron warned before switching his focus to Kip. "Get back in the car, Kip."

Her steps didn't slow. If anything, her pace increased. "No. Don't hurt him."

The panic in Kip's tone had Cameron searching her face for answers. The sheer terror in her eyes shocked him senseless long enough for Kip to throw herself on Josh before Cameron could intervene. Wrapping herself around him like a monkey, Kip snaked her arms and legs around him, protecting as much of Josh as possible. She even went as far as cupping the back of the man's head, blocking the barrel of Cameron's gun.

"No, Cameron. You can't do this to me. Please? You can't."

Fury replaced his shock. How could she protect the man? "Move, Kip. I just caught Josh sneaking out of your home. He's been following you everywhere for months. There's no telling what he's capable of."

A sob tore from Kip's throat, sounding as if her soul was ripping from her chest. Her pain was almost tangible, rocking Cameron on his heels.

"No," she whispered. "Please, Cameron."

Tears streamed down her face. He lowered his weapon and took a step back. So this was how it was. She loved Josh. How had he missed it? She brushed her fingers through Josh's hair, completely focused on the man now that Cameron was no longer holding a gun to his head. Her hands ran down his sides.

"Are you hurt? Oh my God, Jozsua.

Are you okay?"

"I'm fine, baby. It's okay. Take a breath. Breathe with me."

Cameron couldn't tear his eyes away as Josh's chest rose, inhaling deeply as he held Kip's gaze, attempting to lure her into a normal breathing pattern and calm her panic. The thick Russian accent coming from Josh's lips seemed so unnatural, Cameron's mind refused to work. The whole scene felt surreal. He expected to wake up at any moment and leave the crazy dream behind.

Josh swiped at Kip's tears. Cameron swore he heard his heart shatter. She'd risked her life for Josh and allowed him to comfort her. It was as if Cameron had disappeared. He wanted to be angry but his chest hurt too badly. Once she was assured Josh was unharmed, Kip finally focused on Cameron. There was no way she couldn't see his heart breaking. Her face hardened, making things worse. Keeping her eyes locked on him, Kip came to her feet. She ate up the distance between them. If Cameron thought he couldn't be any more surprised by the night's event, he was wrong. She punched him in the arm.

"How dare you? I've lost everyone and everything." More tears fell. She swiped at them angrily. "How could you even think of taking my brother from me as well?"

Cameron opened his mouth, intent on defending himself until her words sank in. "Your brother?"

Kip threw her hands up. "Yes! My baby brother. Who the fuck even does that to someone they're supposed to care about?"

Josh stumbled to his feet. Cameron

switched his gaze between them, doing his best to fit the mismatched pieces together in his head.

"Your brother?" he repeated, incapable of grasping the concept.

Josh moved to stand behind her, bracing his hands on her shoulders. He looked resigned.

"Don't call me your baby brother. I'm only six months younger than you are," Josh said, sounding as stoic as he looked.

Cameron shook his head. Their words didn't make sense. Even as mentally fucked as he was, he knew the math didn't match their claim.

Kip shushed Josh. "I'll call you whatever I like. You're Kon's baby brother and therefore you'll always be mine by extension. Deal with it."

"Wait. Wait," Cameron said,

slashing his hand through the air and bringing their argument to an end. "What the fuck? This guy is your brother?"

"In-law," Josh supplied as if his statement cleared up anything at all.

"In-law?" Cameron knew he was repeating everything they said. He just couldn't stop. "I thought you were an only child. I'm just..." He paused, grasping for words. "I'm not following."

Josh rolled his eyes. "I'm her husband's brother, dumbass. It's not that hard to work out."

"What in the hell is going on out here?" Terry said, causing everyone to turn in his direction.

Jade sat on his forearms with her tiny arms wrapped around his neck. Shit. Cameron had been so focused on this bullshit he'd forgotten she was still in the car. She pointed a finger at Josh and flashed a toothy grin.

"Unc Jos."

A luminous smile stretched the man's face. He held out his arms and Jade threw herself in the man's direction. Terry let it happen...as if Jade did so every day. Cameron watched the entire scene play out with a terrible sense of disconnection. Husband. Josh had definitely said husband. It was amazing how a single word was all it took to level everything. His life. His heart. Their future. It was all gone. Scratch that. It had never existed because Kip belonged to another man.

He couldn't look away from her. She had lived with Terry and Brian for as long as he'd known her. No doubt there was a reason for her being there. Perhaps they were separated or God only knows what, but it didn't matter. Kip was someone else's wife and he was an idiot. A fool

172

who'd been lied to even if it was by omission. She'd never given him a choice. Surely, she knew he'd never trespass in someone's marriage. It went against everything he believed in.

"I have to go."

Kip's gaze shot to his. Cameron didn't know what she saw in his face but he didn't miss the pain in hers. It didn't matter. It couldn't because she didn't belong to him. He headed for the car without a backward glance. Terry said his name but Cameron ignored him. The man obviously knew everything and had said nothing. There wasn't a doubt in Cameron's mind. Kip followed on his heels but didn't try to stop him. Without meeting her gaze, he unstrapped Jade's car seat and pulled her bag from the floorboard. A pain hit him in the chest as he handed them to Kip.

With his door open, Cameron froze. He wouldn't see her again after tonight. That thought alone nearly buckled his knees but it was over. As much as he wanted to leave without exposing himself any more than he already had, Cameron knew if he didn't say what he needed to say, the words would haunt him for the rest of his life. Gathering his pain to shield his heart, Cameron finally met her gaze. It hurt. Her green eyes were still every bit as beautiful even though they belonged to a liar.

"I love you."

She flinched at his confession but didn't look away.

"The moment we met, I knew I would but I also knew someone like me could never hold on to someone like you. You seemed too good to be true. I tried to fight it until the day I couldn't any longer.

But you know what? I was right. You were too good to be true." He glanced away, hoping to escape the hurt showing in her eyes. "What's his name?" Goddamn. He wanted to kick himself for asking. Cameron had to know. He needed it to feel real. A name would make him real.

"Konstantin."

She said his name so quietly without an ounce of explanation or pretending she didn't understand his fury. Unfortunately, the fact she didn't attempt to defend herself only pissed him off more, making him want to lash out.

"I suppose this is for the best. Wanting to be with you has driven me to do things I would never have considered doing. I've become jealous and obsessive." Hardening his heart, he met her stare. "Loving you has made me into a bad person, always looking for the worst in everyone around you in hopes of keeping you and Jade to myself. I don't want to be that person any longer."

Kip drew back as if he'd slapped her. It felt that way to him as well. He didn't take it back. Never in a million years would he have pursued someone's wife. Kip had stolen his free will in the matter and broken his heart along the way. He didn't know where to put that.

"I'm sorry." Her voice came out in a croak but she didn't offer more. Instead, she turned away, accepting the judgment he'd passed.

* * * * *

Cameron was a loss Kip didn't know how to handle. Since the day she came to town, he'd been by her side. Her daughter loved Terry and Brian. The pair spoiled Jade rotten. They stayed up late nights when Jade was sick and went to doctor appointments but they also had each other. While Terry had been hospitalized, undergoing treatment for his non-Hodgkin's, she'd been in the late stages of pregnancy and alone. Cameron had been the one to go on late-night ice-cream runs. He'd held her hand when she was scared. He'd also been the first person to hold Jade in the hospital. Sometimes that knowledge threatened to take her knees out from beneath her.

There was no way Kip could hold back the tears. It felt like years since she'd smiled and meant it. As much as she'd wanted to find the words to make Cameron stay, there was nothing. Thankfully God had taken an ounce of mercy on her, and Jade had been content to hang with Josh. Kip couldn't look at anyone. Even in Cameron's fury, he'd played the gentleman, pulling out her car seat and Jade's bag, making sure Kip had everything she needed. Then he was gone. Just like that, they were done. The memory of the hurt in his eyes was killing her. Her stomach churned. The warm streams of tears rolling down her cheeks seemed to have no end. She'd long passed trying to swipe them away. Tomorrow, she would put her heart back in its box where it belonged. She shouldn't have tried to piece it together and give it new life to begin with.

"Do you want to talk about it?"

Kip continued putting away Jade's things without bothering to glance Terry's way. She wasn't surprised he was there. She would've been more shocked if he wasn't.

"There's nothing to say. He wouldn't let Josh be until I told him the truth. Now he knows. He's done with me."

Cameron was smart. It had only been a matter of time. Even if she hadn't lost her temper and said the words, he would've puzzled things out eventually. When she'd seen the gun pressed to Josh's head, something inside her had snapped. She couldn't handle anything happening to him. She'd promised Konstantin.

"Damn. I told Josh he needed to do a better job of staying out of sight. Cameron's too good at what he does," Terry said, sounding as if the words were meant more for himself than her. "You know, Cameron looks at you the way I imagine I look at Brian. He'll—"

Whatever he planned to say, Kip couldn't listen to it. Even her skin felt raw and exposed. Turning her head, she finally met his stare, cutting off his speech. For a moment, she let him see it all—the emptiness. Her soul. "He said I make him a bad person."

Kip's voice broke on the final word. A fresh wave of tears knocked the air from her lungs. She tried to breathe but nothing happened. The pain was too heavy. Her life was too hard. The world tilted as Terry swept her into his arms. She wanted to fight. It wasn't fair for Cameron to mean so much to her when she knew she couldn't keep him. Her heart was torn to strips. When Terry climbed into her bed and settled her in his arms, even the beating of his heart couldn't take away the sting. This was hell. Cameron was right to walk away. Love had made her a bad person a long time ago. If there was any chance he could be spared, she wanted that for him. He deserved rainbows and sunshine. That wasn't her. It would never be her.

*

Tears pooled in the center of Terry's chest, soaking through his shirt and coating his skin. He hated when Kip cried. It seemed as if she hurt way more than she smiled. His throat swelled. Life had been more than cruel to her. He'd tried to help carry her burden, understanding better than most the pain she was silently forced to carry. There were no good choices—only choices. He'd known Cameron for years. They'd trained together through Cameron's rehabilitation. He'd seen the man at his lowest and known Cameron was at his highest when he met Kip by the way he looked at her. At any time, Terry could've discouraged the man but he'd done the opposite. Kip and Cameron needed each other. Although Kip's strength made a mockery of most men he knew, Terry also recognized the exhaustion in her eyes. Jade was the only thing holding her together. This was one blow too many.

Millions of times, he'd searched his mind, wondering if there was another path. There wasn't. Life had a way of ripping away a person's rose-colored glasses, leaving them an unhindered view of a bleak existence. He couldn't protect her from this. Terry had only seen her broken once before. It was two times too many. Kip's breath shuddered but her tears had stopped. She'd fallen asleep crying. He fucking hated that. Rage boiled beneath his skin.

His jaw popped in his fury. It was unacceptable. He'd let Cameron into her life, trusted him. Easing his arm from beneath Kip's head, Terry ground his teeth. If Cameron wanted to throw all this away, he was a goddamn fool. Kip snuffled in her sleep as he covered her with a blanket from the end of the bed. The sound only solidified his anger. All the people under his roof were his responsibility—his family. No one hurt them.

* * * * *

Cameron's front door shook beneath the fury of the pounding coming from the other side. He checked the peephole, not surprised to see Terry. Cameron had been waiting for the other shoe to drop. The instant he opened the door, Terry was on him. The door slammed behind Terry and Cameron found his back pressed against it before he could even brace for an attack. The scary version of Terry, the one Cameron had seen inside Warehouse, stared at him now. All signs of the man Cameron called friend were gone.

"She makes you a bad person, huh?"

Cameron squeezed his eyes shut at the rage in Terry's voice. It was nothing compared to the anger he felt toward himself. The words sickened him even more now than the moment they'd fallen from his lips and he'd known he could never take them back. It was insane how one small statement had transformed him into something he couldn't stomach.

"I didn't intend to sign on to be anyone's pet."

Terry shoved away from him. "That's fucking stupid. Kip wouldn't have wasted her time on you if she didn't care. Come on, man. You've been there for every step since Kip came to town. Has she been parading men through her bedroom? Hell, before you finally wised up and staked a claim, we could barely pry her out of the house."

The truth behind Cameron's pain

stared him in the face at Terry's words. She'd made Cameron believe she meant every touch—that he was special. It was cruel. She made him feel powerful—whole.

"She'll never belong to me." As the confession left him, Cameron's mind raged against it. For a moment, he'd held the world. His life had been transformed the night he'd chosen to throw himself on top of an Afghani child, hoping to save the boy's life. He'd failed and everything had changed. Then he'd met Kip and for the first time in years, he'd dared to dream. "Konstantin is her husband, and I'm assuming Jade's father. I can't compete. It wouldn't be right for me to try." And he'd failed again, he silently added.

A line appeared between Terry's eyes. Confusion crowded his features. "Cameron, Konstantin is dead. He died a month before Jade was born."

"I don't understand." He really didn't. There were too many questions. Not that Cameron had given Kip much of a chance to defend herself. But she'd certainly had time to say her husband was dead. "She said nothing." She'd merely stood there and taken his rage as if she'd earned it.

Terry's eyes fell closed and he turned away.

"Tell me everything," Cameron said, demanding of Terry what Kip had denied Cameron.

*

Terry dug the heels of his hands into his eye sockets until stars burst behind his lids. No matter how hard he fought, some memories burned so brightly in his mind he thought he'd go blind when they hit. Kip said she'd told Cameron the truth. He'd come here, expecting the man knew it all. Fuck. Even though it felt like yesterday, Terry never wanted to relive it.

*"One of Russia's top mafia leaders, Konstantin Danshov, was found dead..." The words continued playing through Terry's mind, making him insane. He had to get to Kip. Walking the fine line between feeding his panic and keeping to the speed limit was killing him. Whatever he did, Terry could not get pulled over. That was time he didn't have to spare. The fifteen minutes it took him to get across town felt closer to hours. There was a weight sitting on his throat, choking the life from him. His eyes burned. The road blurred. He had to hold his shit together. Goddamn it. Konstantin. Bile rose in his throat.*

*When the house finally came into view, Terry knew it was bad. Josh stood in the driveway. The front door stood open as if awaiting Terry's arrival. As he stepped* from the car, his and Josh's eyes met before dancing away. Before now, they'd pretended not to know who Josh truly was. He'd simply stayed in the background, playing along with everyone's beliefs he was the father of Kip's baby while silently protecting her. Considering the man's less than legal ties, the ruse was best for everyone. In the public's eyes, Josh's crimes were nothing in comparison to Kon's. Kip's child would never be safe if anyone learned she was part of the Danshov family. The second he reached the front steps Terry could hear Kip's screams.

Broken glass littered the kitchen. Following the line of debris and sound of crying, Terry found Kip inside one of the back bedrooms. Brian had her arms locked to her sides, holding her to his chest, doing his best to keep her from harming herself or the baby she carried. Her heart-wrenching *cries came from the soul. Red locks of hair clung to her face, hiding it from him. Brian's face was void of all emotion—except for his eyes. Her pain was killing him.*

*Terry didn't hesitate. Closing the distance between them, he pushed Kip's hair away and held her face between his hands, forcing her to meet his stare. Her eyes looked crazed. He knew she recognized his devastation. Konstantin had given him back his life, ensuring he could spend it with Brian. There was no repaying that and now he was gone. The fight bled from Kip's body. She went limp in Terry's arms. A loud sob tore from her throat, crushing his heart.*

*"I've got you, angel," he whispered, pushing the words past the lump in his throat. "You have to calm down. Please think of Kon's baby." Bending, Terry swept Kip into his arms before focusing on Brian.*

*The man looked ragged from the battle. He'd been sitting by Terry's hospital bed for months and they'd only recently felt some sense of normalcy again. This could have been Brian's life. This is what his pain would've looked like if Terry hadn't survived. For a moment, they simply stared at one another, devastated. There was no fixing this.*

*"Make Josh come inside before someone calls the cops," he said, attempting to take control of what he could.*

*With a nod, Brian was off. Konstantin was gone. Everything Kip had given back to Brian and Terry was gone for her.*

Even now, Terry didn't know how to process that. But for a moment, he'd believed she might have a shot at a new life. If there was a chance he could help her have it, he'd have to tell Cameron everything.

"You won't like it."

Cameron snorted. "I don't like it now. How much worse could it be?"

"Konstantin Danshov."

An amused-sounding chuckle filled the air. "That Russian hockey player who turned out to be some sort of mafia drug lord, that Konstantin Danshov?"

Terry didn't laugh. Cameron sobered. "Are you serious?"

Terry didn't bother answering. He simply stared at Cameron, waiting for him to accept the truth. Cameron sat.

"Holy shit. You are serious. But Kip is so...Kip-like. How in the hell did she end up married to that guy?"

A spark of anger ignited in Terry's chest. "That guy loved Kip. He might not have been your definition of a good man but he was a good man. That guy saved my life so be careful how you judge."

*

Cameron had never been more confused in his life. Of all the things in the world Terry could've possibly told him, this news wasn't even on Cameron's radar. When he tried to picture what he could remember of the headlines about Konstantin, Cameron didn't remember anything about a wife but he remembered little, period. He might have forgotten the man's name if it hadn't been such a huge story. Konstantin had saved Terry's life? How was such a thing even possible? From what Cameron understood, Konstantin had been deported years ago. For the sake of his sanity alone, Cameron focused on one thing at a time.

"The last I remember hearing of him, he'd been deported. I didn't know he'd died. What happened to him?"

Terry paced away. He moved to the window and glanced outside. Cameron couldn't decide if Terry was trying to avoid the question or gathering his thoughts.

"He failed," Terry said after a minute without meeting Cameron's stare. "It was his job to be here and he got caught. It was only a matter of time before that mistake came back to haunt him so he sent Josh to watch over Kip." Terry snorted. "Not that she makes it easy for him."

In spite of the humor in Terry's tone as he said those final words, when he turned, Cameron saw a different story in Terry's eyes. There was so much more to all of this than Cameron would ever know. Perhaps he didn't want to know. Cameron had lived his entire life doing what was good and right, even when it wasn't easy and it cost him everything. Konstantin Danshov didn't stand for any of those things.

"I know you're angry about everything when it comes to Josh but he's Kip's family. Jade and Josh are all she has." Terry made a helpless gesture. "I get Josh better than anyone can. We're exactly the same. He's the brother who lived. It's a cruel joke to be the one left behind, and it makes Josh a dangerous person to have standing between you and her. Kip and Jade are all the man has left of a brother who looked after him and loved him like a father would have done. He'll never stop protecting that link to a life lost and I have to respect him for that. You should too if you really love Kip. I also get that your pride is hurt because Kip didn't confide in you but she couldn't tell you. You have to see that. If anyone knew Jade was Kon's daughter, she'd live in the spotlight for the rest of her life. As the daughter of a deadbeat dad...well, that happens every day. No one will look too closely. This is the only way Kip can be free, and if Josh stays as he is, there's no reason for anyone to question the identity he lives under. Everyone can move on with their lives. Kip couldn't jeopardize their positions just to keep you from getting pissed all the time. Konstantin left her behind, trading his life so she could live a normal life. If your bruised pride protected that sacrifice, I can't be sorry and she shouldn't have to be either. He's gone and Kip fell in love with you. Don't be stupid and throw that away."

Cameron heard every word. On the surface, it made sense. To Cameron's heart, Kip's lies were shredding him to pieces. He'd exposed himself to her in a way he'd never done before. A fucking drug lord. He was a cop—a former soldier.

Where did he go with that?

*

Kip's eyes flew open. She stared at the empty spot beside her, not bothering to turn her head to ensure she was alone. She already knew. No one would be there. It was the way of things. Fumbling around, she found her phone among the sheets and pulled up her voicemail. With it pressed to her ear, she let Konstantin's final message soothe her the way it always did. In the end, this was all she had.

"I miss you, my Kipley. Say the word and I'll send for you."

There was a long pause. It was exactly three seconds, Kipley knew. She'd listened to this message a million times since his death. She knew exactly when he'd speak again and what he'd say, like a song she'd sung along with too many times.

"It sits on my chest," Konstantin said, tearing at her soul as always. "But you don't want this life. I crave you, Kipley. Every day. Underneath me and moaning my name." Konstantin drew an unsteady breath. "I'm only content when your juices are coating every inch of my skin. The way your skin tastes as you come against my lips is the most addictive flavor in the world. Press your palm against your mound, Kip, and listen to my voice. Let me pretend for a little while it's me. I'm sending Josh to you. Let him take care of you, Kipley. I can't be there with you. Don't shut him out. I love you, my angel."

Kip restarted the message and listened to it from the beginning.

*Turning inside herself, Kip drew a deep breath through her nose, absorbing the moment. Konstantin's warm grip held her by the nape, keeping her locked in place. As her eyes slowly opened, she took in the vision of Konstantin only inches away. They kept their foreheads pressed together as if the small connection could keep them from ever being separated. This was her husband. A wave of love and longing so deep she thought she might drown washed over her. A set of blue eyes stared back at her. If there was anyone in the world more beautiful than him, she'd never heard the tale.*

*"Damn. I love you so much."*

*Her nose stung at Konstantin's claim. Life was cruel. All they'd ever wanted was to be together. A normal life was always just out of reach.*

*"Kip and Kon. Kon and Kip. That's freaking adorable," Jozsua said in a singsong voice, interrupting their moment.*

*"Shut it, Jozsua," Kon growled without looking away. The way his eyes*

*crinkled in the corners said more than his tone. He wasn't bothered. "That is pretty freaking cute though."*

"I see you're torturing yourself again."

The memory disappeared. Kip glanced over her shoulder to find Josh leaning against the doorframe with his arms crossed over his chest and his feet crossed at the ankles as if he'd been there a while.

She looked away. "No." Tucking the phone beneath her, she made room for Josh next to her. "I don't want to forget. Sometimes he starts to slip away and I hate myself for it."

Josh stretched out beside her. On his side, with his arms pillowing his head, Josh stared at her in silence. She always wondered what he saw when he looked at her. It was rare for Josh to let his guard down but when he did, he reminded her so much of Konstantin. Kip's stomach churned. Josh had left the love of his life behind to protect her. Sometimes, it was like she was a disease, stealing everything good from the people she loved the most.

"How do you do it, Jozsua? How do you get up every day, knowing Dmitry is out there, and you'll never be together again, because of this stupid fucking life that's been thrust upon us? Why don't you hate me?"

"Do you remember the time that Canadian guy who played on Kon's team tried hitting on you?" Josh asked, avoiding her questions. "He spoke more French than English and swore you should be his because he could woo you with the words of love."

A burble of laughter rose in Kip's throat. She knew Josh was trying to distract her, but she also knew the exact night he described and Josh did an amazing impression of the guy's way of speaking. She hadn't understood half of what the man had said but she remembered everything Konstantin said.

"Kon stood in a chair and professed his undying love for me to everyone within shouting distance."

"And their neighbors," Josh added with a chuckle. "He refused to stop singing your praises, promising to stay there until he withered away of old age."

"Or starved to death," Kip interjected.

"Whichever came first," he agreed. "Until you swore you'd never been more thoroughly wooed."

She shook her head at the memory. "Damn. He was outrageous."

Josh's foot shifted, slipping between

hers as he moved closer until barely an inch separated them. "He was crazy over you. Kon didn't give a fuck what anyone else thought of him. He just wanted to hear you laugh. I can't tell you how many times he told me you were the only thing he possessed that couldn't be replaced."

Kip swallowed, trying to hold her every emotion on the inside. Josh wasn't finished.

"He wouldn't like knowing you're sad."

"I know."

"You have to find a way to be happy."

"I know." She could hear herself but those two words were all she had. Konstantin would've hated knowing she hurt and part of her couldn't let him go. That was the real reason she'd never said the words to Cameron. If she did,

Konstantin would really be gone.

"What'll it take, Kip? Do I need to smash shit until you promise you'll heal? Tell me how I can fix this?"

"You can't. It has to be me."

"I'm sorry if I fucked things up with Cameron. You should've let him shoot me."

A wry smile twisted Kip's lips. "There's no way in hell I'd let anyone hurt you and it's not your fault he's more observant than most. You've shadowed me for years with no one spotting you. When I let you watch over me, that is."

The smile exploding across Josh's face eased some of the tightness in her chest. Loss hadn't killed her yet. There wasn't much hope it would this time either.

# Chapter Six

Kip jabbed the straw into the tiny hole at the top of the juice box with way more force than necessary. Unfortunately, her fit ended with her shirt covered in a stream of sticky, apple-flavored sugar water. She was restless and agitated. Three days had passed since Cameron walked away. In all the time she'd known him, they'd never gone that long without speaking. There'd been a few times over the past three days when she'd almost caved and texted him. His final words still rang in her ears and they stopped her every time. He was done with her and Kip would have to accept it.

Jade stood with her hands braced on the edge of the entertainment center and Kip had given up trying to move her away from the TV. If she ended up needing glasses, Kip would be sure to remind her of this exhausting moment. Kip's skin crawled with the need to do something. Anything. The inside of her head felt like spring fever. Something had been set free from hibernation, driving her to act. Jade giggled, refusing to accept the drink Kip offered.

"Horsey. I pet horsey," Jade babbled as she tried climbing the entertainment center. Kip glanced at the TV. A horse, the same color as Butter, filled the screen and Jade was determined to get her. Lifting Jade into her arms, Kip stared into space as Jade attempted to pet the horse through the screen. There would be sticky fingerprints all over it after she got through, but no one in their home cared.

Something shifted in Kip's chest. A veil lifted away. Her gaze moved to Jade. Konstantin's soft blond curls and gorgeous blue eyes stared back at her. His daughter possessed the same sense of devilry. She was a mini version of him in almost every way. They needed no one else. An image of Cameron floated through her mind. Kip pushed it away as a wave of longing and love overcame her, closely followed by regret. She wasn't a bad person. Neither was Konstantin. He'd had no more control over the family he'd been born into than anyone else on the planet and together they'd created a beautiful daughter. Jade's laughter should've filled their home. Their daughter should've had the chance to know the man who gave her life and loved her even though they'd never meet. Jade should be free to know his name.

Kip set Jade on the floor, ensuring she was content with her juice box before heading for her room. She didn't hesitate or stop to think it through. It was time. With a tug, she slid the mattress down, exposing the box springs underneath. Running her fingers along the edge, she found the long metal piece that shouldn't have been there. When she pulled on it, a section popped away, revealing the hidden compartment inside and the black bag she'd kept hidden. For a moment, she stared down at it, unable to bring herself to touch it. When she finally reached for it, her hands shook. It was time, she reminded herself. Konstantin always meant for her to use it. Once it was in her hands, her resolve set in. She was doing the right thing.

Her phone came next. It was the hardest. The desire to listen to Konstantin's voice one more time before leaving it behind was crippling. In the end, she knew there wasn't time. She'd do this now or she'd lose her nerve. With the notebook app open, she typed a quick note to Josh, letting him know where she was headed before scrambling the phone. He was the only person who knew the code. She set it on the nightstand, her fingers hovering over the device. Once she walked away, she'd never hear Konstantin's voice again. He was gone. Swallowing past the lump in her throat, Kip took a step back. It was time.

"Jade, let's find your shoes, baby."

\* \* \* \* \*

It took three weeks for Cameron to accept the truth. He couldn't live without Kip. No matter how he plotted, he couldn't settle on how to apologize. Shit. He couldn't take back the things he'd said. The problem wasn't her or the secrets she'd kept. It was him. Cameron had searched his soul and didn't like what he'd seen. A part of him had enjoyed painting Josh as the villain. If he could save Kip, then there'd be an explanation as to why she wanted him. Without that, she was with him because she wanted to be, and that made no sense. Even he didn't like being with him. Three weeks without her brought an unexpected realization—it didn't fucking matter why she wanted him. For some cosmic, unforeseen reason, she'd chosen him. Instead of searching for holes in her logic, he should've held on for dear life.

Unfortunately, this newfound understanding came with another ugly truth—he didn't know how to win her back. Apologizing wouldn't be enough. Cameron couldn't claim he wasn't upset she'd kept things from him but in the grand scheme of things, it mattered not at all. It was also true he might not ever see Konstantin Danshov in the light she and

Terry did, but Terry was right. The man was dead. No matter how Cameron chased things around in his head, his thoughts always came back to one place—he needed help if he was going to make this right.

The inside of Grid Iron was like most high-dollar fitness centers—built to keep non-members at bay. A front desk and glass double doors separated the front entry from the gym. He didn't have a membership but that hadn't stopped him in the past. Luckily, Ryan's sister, Kerry, was the one keeping everyone in line. Cameron could only hope his black disposition didn't show through and keep him out. She was the type to do as she pleased. If it didn't please her to let him in, he wouldn't be going.

The place was open twenty-four hours and it didn't occur to Cameron she might not be there until his fingers closed around the handle of Grid Iron's front door. The sudden wave of panic overcoming him didn't pass until he set eyes on the curvy brunette behind the desk. Thank God. Pasting on a fake smile, Cameron prayed he could do this. Kerry waved at him as he cleared the threshold.

"Who's this cutie?" Cameron asked, leaning over the top of her desk to check out the fat and obviously newly born baby sleeping on Kerry's chest. A cap covered his head, hiding all but his chubby cheeks and half-open mouth from sight.

"Oh wow. I forgot you haven't met my awesome nephew. This is Dante. He's the coolest."

Kerry's excitement was catching. In spite of his nervousness and shit mood, he couldn't help but smile.

"He's adorable. Knox and Mandy's?" She'd said nephew and Cameron knew

Ryan didn't have kids. It was an educated guess.

"Nah. Knox and Mandy are a lot like Dane and me. They're pretty happy with their empty nest. This little dude belongs to Rhys and Asher. They hired a surrogate a while back. Only the family knew because they were nervous it would fall through or something would go wrong, but everything went great. Rhys is back there somewhere, sparring with Knox today, and I get to hang out with my favorite nephew."

"Isn't he your only nephew?"

Kerry shot him an irritated look and tried covering Dante's ears. "Hush. He's still my favorite. What bring you by today anyhow?"

"I had some time to kill and was hoping to catch Ryan and Max between classes." She glanced at the clock over his shoulder. "You're right on time then. They've got about twenty minutes until their next batch of students roll in. Do you remember where to go?"

"Turn right and head for the back."

Kerry smiled as if he'd passed a test. "You got it. If they're not in the classroom yet, they will be within the next few minutes so you shouldn't miss them."

He tried hiding his relief as he headed for the door. "Thanks, Kerry."

"Think nothing of it. I'd do a lot of things for a sexy man with handcuffs."

Only the fact that his back was turned saved him from showing his shock. He blinked, shaking his head. The wicked chuckle following him through the door and into the club cleared things up. He had indeed heard her right.

Cameron nodded at a few familiar faces along the way. Thankfully, he spotted Ryan and Max warming up inside the classroom before he reached the door. Cameron had little time and didn't know where to start. As it turned out, he didn't need to know.

"Things get too real for you?" Ryan asked with a smirk the second Cameron's ass hit the chair.

"I take it you've seen Kip."

Max and Ryan nodded. Ryan's smirk never faltered. Cameron got the feeling the man was pissed. That didn't stop Cameron from wanting to wipe the knowing smile from Ryan's face. Cameron should've known better than to come here. How could he expect them to understand? He started to move to his feet. Max's hand landed on Cameron's shoulder, pushing him back down. He could've resisted but Ryan's expression turned serious, holding Cameron enthralled. Max was usually the somber one. Cameron wanted to hear their thoughts. Max was the first to break.

"Do you think anyone could touch our love?" he asked, motioning between himself and Ryan. "This is the real fucking deal."

"I know it is," Cameron said, meaning it. He did know. If anyone loved each other from the soul, it was Max and Ryan.

"You could've fucking fooled me. You're acting like we're nothing more than a pair of man-whores who'll screw around with anyone for shits and giggles—as if Ryan could ever be replaced."

Confusion crowded Cameron's brain. "What the fuck are you talking about? I didn't say any of that."

"But Ryan kissed Kip."

Cameron made a helpless gesture, incapable of grasping Max's point or this entire conversation for that matter. "So?"

Max growled. "So he doesn't intend to leave me for her. It was physical."

"I'm aware," Cameron said slowly, wondering if he'd suffered some sort of psychotic break with reality.

"Then I'm having a hard fucking time understanding why you can't understand there was a physical relationship between Kip and Josh that isn't relative any longer."

Oh. Of course, they wouldn't know the truth.

"Instead of letting that shit go and realizing he's the dumb fuck who gave up a life with her, you're treating Kip as if she should be the saint you've painted her to be in your mind. Dude. That's not fair. Last we saw, you were enjoying kinky Kip just fine."

"I don't want her to be a saint."

Really. He didn't know what else to say. Their lecture was no longer relevant but it was enlightening.

Max ran his hands through his hair. "Then what in the hell are you doing? I know you love her."

"I do."

"Then how could you let her get away? Trust me on this," Max begged. "You don't want to get so caught up in a box you didn't label that you lose everything that matters. The only voice in your head that matters is yours and right now, your voice is the town idiot. Kip fucking loved you."

Even though Max had no freaking idea what was going on he still made sense. Cameron had labeled himself unworthy and given up on a normal life. None of it mattered. Kip had loved him and he didn't give a shit if life was ordinary as long as she was in it.

"Well, fuck." He should've just apologized instead of trying to come up with some elaborate scheme to win her back. A wry smile twisted Cameron's lips. He always overthought things. "I appreciate the pep talk. I guess I'd better head out before Kip shows up for her lesson." Cameron would beg for her forgiveness but not here.

"Um." Max and Ryan exchanged glances. "When was the last time you talked to Kip?"

The muscles in Cameron's stomach tightened at Ryan's tone. There was something going on. "It's been a while. Why?"

Another look passed between the men.

"Kip isn't coming in today," Max answered.

"Or any day," Ryan added. "She dropped our class."

Cameron's brow drew tight. "But she loves your class." He didn't like to look too closely at why. He imagined it was for the same reason all women loved their class. "Why would she drop out?"

Max shook his head. "I thought you knew. When you walked in here looking all brokenhearted, I thought that's what you were here about."

"I came here to ask a favor but changed my mind." Cameron swiped his hands over his face. "Seriously? What the fuck is going on?"

"Kip's gone. She said it was time for her and Jade to make a fresh start."

The room darkened at the corners of his vision. "What?" His voice sounded hollow even to his ears.

Max and Ryan both nodded but it

was Max who spoke up.

"Brian and Terry were brokenhearted, but they understand she needs to live her life. Not to mention they're off traveling more than half the time now that Brian's mid-weight champion, and Kip was all alone in that big-ass house."

Cameron didn't understand. Really. He didn't. "Where did she go?"

Both men shrugged.

"All she said was she was used to living on the road and missed seeing the world. Apparently Jade's recent first experience with some horses made Kip realize how much Jade was missing. I'm sure Brian and Terry know where she's gone but they left for Germany yesterday." Ryan gave Cameron's shoulder a pat, as if it softened the blow of his words. "I'm sorry, dude. It didn't occur to me you didn't know. I figured even though the two of you'd fallen out, since you'd been close for so long, you'd know where she was. I was trying to convince you to go after her, not kick you while you're down."

Cameron nodded. Even to him it felt forced. He knew Max wouldn't intentionally hurt anyone. Somehow, Cameron's lips formed some semblance of a goodbye and his feet automatically carried him back to his car. Cameron didn't remember a second of it. Minutes passed, turning into an hour as Cameron sat behind the wheel, staring at nothing. She was gone... Kip and Jade—they were...gone. His eyes fell closed. He'd lost everything.

As his eyes opened, he caught sight of a familiar figure moving across the parking lot. Josh was headed for the door of Grid Iron. Why wasn't he with Kip?

Before Cameron could consider the ramifications of his actions, he was out of the car and heading in the man's direction.

"Where are they?"

Josh cast a glance over his shoulder at Cameron's question but kept walking. "I don't know what you mean?"

"Kip and Jade."

Josh didn't back down. "Nope. Doesn't ring a bell."

Cameron checked his surroundings, ensuring no one was watching before snagging the back of Josh's shirt. The ache blooming in the center of his chest gave Cameron superhuman strength. With a flick of his wrist, he spun Josh around and slammed him against the brick of the building. Pinning him in place, Cameron got in Josh's face. "Let me jog your memory,

Jozsua."

Josh shoved him away. "Don't call me by that name."

An evil smile pulled at Cameron's lips. "I know all about you, Jozsua Danshov. If you don't tell me where Kip has gone, I'll stand on the hood of my car and scream your real name until I'm sure everyone in Vegas knows as well."

In spite of Cameron's threat, Josh's mouth lifted in one corner. "Konstantin would've loved you."

"I'm not sure that's true but I need to know where they are."

Josh's smirk transformed into a huge grin. "You didn't know him. A show like that on Kip's behalf would've made him proud." Josh's expression hardened. "You won't like it."

"I'm not surprised."

"There's no going back from here,

cop."

"There was never any going back," Cameron said, never meaning anything more in his life. From the moment he set eyes on Kip, he'd known his life would change forever. He was ready.

"Konstantin is Jade's father. She deserves to be free to love him without judgment. If you can't offer that, then you need to stay away from them."

"I know," Cameron agreed, surprised to find the idea didn't bother him at all. It had to be that way.

"The same goes for me. She's a part of my brother and I won't give her up."

"You're a smart man."

Josh's eyes flashed. Cameron glimpsed something deadly inside Josh. He was a man with demons.

"If you ever expose her, they'll never find your body."

Cameron didn't doubt him. "I wouldn't expect anything less," he agreed, more than willing to meet those terms. Cameron would die for her. He really would.

# Chapter Seven

Ryan and Max were a pair of liars. Cameron shouldn't have been surprised. They'd openly admitted to being some of the best at manipulating people into doing what they wanted. In this case, their manipulations aligned with what Cameron wanted as well. Lucky for them he wouldn't need to kill them both. Kip had left, in a manner of speaking—one hour off Highway 11 and down a dirt road. If she really had dropped the men's self-defense class, it was because it was damn inconvenient. Cameron had to backtrack three times before he found the place. Once he did, he couldn't figure out how he'd missed it. The place was freaking huge.

The house itself wasn't ostentatious but it was located on a little piece of mountain spring heaven that had to have cost millions. For all that, Kip's security system sucked. Cameron was inside within two minutes with no one the wiser. Knocking didn't work for his purposes. As stubborn as Kip could be, he was likely to stand on her front porch until the end of time.

While he waited for her to discover his presence, Cameron took a stroll through the house. There was no way in hell she'd recently purchased this place. There were no boxes and a few of the pictures hanging on the walls had dust on the frames. It was another mystery for him to solve. He recognized a few of the toys in the living room as belonging to Jade. An ache bloomed in his chest. He couldn't fail. Kip and Jade meant too much.

As quietly as possible, he searched the front rooms. Everything was silent.

There was a small bathroom that was obviously meant for guests and an empty bedroom directly off the living room. A huge, country-style kitchen flanked the other side but other than the hum of the refrigerator, the room was quiet. As he passed a set of French doors, he spotted the sparkling-blue water of an in-ground pool, but there was no sign of Kip outside. He hit the hallway, glancing inside each room as he passed. A trashed bedroom called him inside. It was obvious a man lived there. Cameron's heart fell. He didn't hesitate before shifting through the room's contents in search of the man's identity. A few framed snapshots on the dresser cleared things up. Josh... With a resigned sigh, Cameron headed back down the hall. He should've known.

A closed door caught his eye and Cameron's pulse beat in his ears. He held his breath as he eased it open, bracing for Kip to attack. It was an office. Releasing his breath, Cameron eased inside. There were dozens of trophies and autographed photos of famous hockey players. Konstantin filled every inch of the room. Cameron had a vague image of the man in his mind from the news and seeing him on TV for the games. Those memories didn't prepare him for seeing Kon's face now. He was larger than life. The blue eyes and bright smile gleaming in every picture spoke volumes about his personality. He was a mountain of a man who towered over everyone in every shot. It was the pictures of him and Kip that drew Cameron closer. They were mesmerizing together. Cameron couldn't look away.

There were no shadows underneath Kip's eyes. She looked innocent and in love. It took Cameron a full five minutes of moving from frame to frame and back again to realize what it was about the pictures that made him accept everything Terry claimed about the man as the truth. In every single shot, Kip smiled at the camera. Konstantin smiled at her. He'd loved her. The knowledge was enough to tighten Cameron's throat. He understood the man then. Cameron had broken into Kip's home, proving there was no length to which he wouldn't go to win her back. Maybe he wasn't as different from Konstantin as he'd thought.

"This was supposed to be our new beginning."

Cameron's heart slammed against the wall of his chest, taking five years from his life. Spinning, he found Kip leaning against the doorframe, watching him. He'd never seen a more beautiful sight.

"He was found in a back alley by an

elderly shopkeeper two weeks before he planned to meet me here with a new identity—just in time for the birth of his daughter. He'd been shot twice in the back of the head, execution style." Her gaze shifted to the photos hanging on the wall. "I've wondered a thousand times how I'll tell our daughter how her father died."

Fuck. It was a hell of a burden. "I don't know."

Kip's focus bounced to his face as if she'd almost forgotten he was there. "Why are you here, Cameron?"

She didn't sound the least bit happy to see him. It hurt. He deserved it. "To tell you I'm sorry."

Kip straightened away from the door. "Well. You've said it. Thanks for stopping by."

Turning her back to him, Kip walked away, leaving him standing in the middle of Konstantin's office without a backward glance. Oh hell no. She wasn't brushing him off that easily. He chased after her.

"I also wanted to hear about Konstantin from your lips," Cameron called at her back. "Terry told me some of it but I want to hear it from you. I deserve that much."

Throwing those last words her way had been a dirty move. He didn't care. She would face him. He would fight. She made it to the living room before turning on him.

"Why, Cameron? Why do you care? I make you a bad person, remember? You should go on with your life and forget you know any of this."

She visibly swallowed, crushing his chest. Her voice came out low as if she felt the same.

"Wash your hands of me and be

clean again."

Goddamn, he wanted to put his fist through the wall. "I love you, Kip. That's something I can't wash away. Let me have this closure."

*

Because her knees didn't want to hold her any longer, Kip sat down on the couch. From the minute she'd spotted Cameron standing in the center of Konstantin's things, she'd barely taken a full breath. How had he found her? It had to be Josh. Why would he sell her out? Kip hadn't thought she could hurt more but seeing Cameron did. It cut deeper than she could put into words. Looking at the man who'd given her hope again, only to snatch it away, was the worst form of torture.

No matter how much it pained her Kip couldn't deny he deserved to hear the words from her. She'd lied by omission and stolen his choices, turning something beautiful into something profane. "Where would you like me to start?"

Cameron sprang forward, claiming the empty spot beside her. "At the beginning. Where were you born? What were you like as a child? How did you come to be where you are? Everything. When you called Josh your brother, I felt as if I was staring at a stranger and I hated it."

The heat radiating from his thigh against hers made her want to cry.

"It seems crazy for me to love someone so much and know nothing about her. I want to know every detail even if you think I won't like it."

Kip wished he would stop saying he loved her, mocking what it should've been and pointing out what she'd lost. She also thought he was crazy for wanting to know anything about her. There were thousands of details about her life he would hate knowing. Maybe it was for the best he did. Staring at the corner of the room, Kip tried to decide where to begin. No matter how hard she tried, she couldn't look at Cameron. The only person who knew the full story of her life was dead. In a way, she always hoped that's where her past would stay. "I was born in Ashwood, Texas. The state took custody of me when I was three when a Sunday school teacher noticed both my legs were covered in cigarette burns."

Cameron made a noise in the back of his throat. It was deadly.

"I don't remember the abuse," Kip added in case he thought she was traumatized. She had more time for that later in life. "I sort of bounced around from home to home with varying degrees of failure. There was one where they had a teenage son who was a little too fond of me, and another where I slept on the floor, starving while they cashed the state's checks."

Jesus. Even to Kip, her voice sounded dead. It was as if she was telling the life story of someone she'd never met, but she was too far in to stop now. "By the time I turned sixteen, I lived in an overcrowded, state-run facility, beyond the age of having any hope of finding a permanent home. I rode it out until they turned me loose at eighteen. Luckily, I found this tiny apartment above a tattoo parlor. It was a rough place but the people who hung out and worked there let me be. A temp agency kept me in odd jobs so the rent was always paid and the owner was happy."

"Damn, Kip. Anything could've

happened to you."

Since he'd lasted longer than she'd expected without getting judgmental, Kip let it slide. She shrugged, still incapable of looking at him. "I guess, depending upon how you look at it, anything did happen to me. One day about six months after I moved in, I was coming home, and this man stepped out of the shop." Kip paused, relishing the memory of seeing Konstantin for the first time. "He was devastating," Kip said with a smile, lacking a more powerful word. "Like a devil wearing an angel's clothes. My feet froze to the pavement. I must've looked like a complete idiot. If so, Konstantin never said as much. We just stared at each other, speechless." Kip shook her head. "I'd never seen a single hockey game. As a matter of fact, I hated all sports equally. Even without knowing who he was, I was star struck. There was just something about him..." Kip trailed off, oddly reluctant to share the rest of that day with anyone. The way Konstantin held her hand, the first time they'd kissed, all those memories were hers.

"What was he like?"

At the genuine curiosity in Cameron's voice, Kip finally looked over. There wasn't an ounce of judgment in his eyes. It loosened the vise on her chest. A snort escaped her.

"Ridiculous," she answered without an ounce of shame. "Seriously, he wasn't anything like what you'd think. Drug lord paints an ominous picture, but no... He was a giant clown. Everywhere he went, laughter followed. For me, it was like heaven. I was addicted. He would be outrageous to the point of being unbearable. My cheeks would ache from smiling. Then at the oddest of times, he'd pause and focus on me. It took my breath every damn time."

Clearing her throat, Kip looked away and swiped her hands down the front of her jeans. "Anyway, by the time I realized there was more to him than I knew, it was as if it wasn't real. I mean, look where I came from. No one gets to choose his or her family, and his was so far away. Konstantin kept me insulated from that world until it crashed down on me. One day, he was just gone and I found myself in the center of this huge shit storm." A wry smile twisted Kip's lips. "He bought our way out of it but our life was over."

Cameron shifted. "Wait. I thought he was deported and they realized too late they'd allowed a major mafia tie to slip through their fingers."

Kip couldn't help it. She laughed. Unfortunately, it wasn't a pleasant sound. Nothing about any of it had been fun for her. "He was married to me and had been for nine years. Not only was Kon legally in this country, there was zero reason he couldn't have been tried here. Deportation was just a scheme to put him back in the hands of his family. Luckily, Josh was still completely under the radar. He was off doing what he does, kicking people's ass for a living. Kon sent him to get me and we hit the road, traveling to all the matches around the country."

"That explains a lot," Cameron said, sounding as if was meant for himself. "Why did he ditch you in Tennessee?"

This time when Kip laughed, she meant it. Poor Josh. She was such a plague on his life. "He didn't. I left him no choice. He'd been at it pretty hard for a few months and he was bored and acting all sulky. Brian was sitting at the bar. I was watching him. He looked like I felt—broken. We'd passed each other several times along the tour and I'd never seen him like that. Josh was eating and I ambushed him. Taking a page from Kon's book, I started yelling at the top of my lungs, accusing Josh of checking out our waitress and claiming he was always screwing around on me." With a chuckle, Kip shook her head. "As long as I live, I'll never forget the look on his face. He didn't know what the hell to do. But he knew from living with Kon, he needed to go along with me if there was any hope of making me stop. I stormed off and he stormed off. Dear God. He was fucking pissed. I've never seen him so furious. Only the fact that Brian took me in saved me from his wrath."

"I can imagine," Cameron said, snagging her attention.

She glanced over, showing an ounce of weakness. "Something drove me that night. I had this overwhelming desire to act. Do something. Anything. It led me to you. There have been days, since Konstantin died, when I didn't think I could stand another second inside my skin. Then I'd remember that I'd met you because of all this and think everything I've been through happened for a reason. Now I realize it was just a series of events and impulsive decisions that led nowhere. How sad for all of us." Kip stood before she exposed any more of her heart. It was already bleeding and raw. "I hope you found what you came looking for and maybe one day you'll think back on this without hating me."

"I could never hate you."

The conviction in his tone gave Kip pause. She searched his gaze. He meant it. A pain shot through her, nearly crippling her. Why wouldn't he leave? "That's nice. You should go before Jade wakes up from her nap. It'll be hard on her to see you again only to have you disappear."

Cameron winced before a look of determination crossed his features. A bad feeling overcame her. He crossed his arms over his chest. His jaw took on a stubborn tilt.

"No."

"What do you mean no?"

A smirk touched his lips. "No," he repeated, drawing out the word as if he was enjoying himself.

Shifting from foot to foot, Kip ran through a list of her options. It wasn't likely she could physically throw him from the house.

"Josh will be home any minute." There. That should piss him off enough to move his ass.

Ignoring her, he felt around beside him. A triumphant light entered his eyes. The footstool popped out and Cameron kicked back, settling in. "So?"

"What do you mean so?" Kip asked, wondering what in the hell was happening. Cameron laced his fingers behind his head. The motion caused his t-shirt to stretch tight across the muscles in his chest. It wasn't fair for him to be so tempting.

"So what if Josh comes home?"

"I don't know," she answered honestly. The bastard smiled. "I want to see Jade."

Kip rubbed her hands together, more nervous than she could remember being in years. "She's sleeping."

His gaze swept down her body, leaving her skin heated. Seriously. It wasn't fair. "Then we have some time alone."

Her hands rose before falling back to her sides. She was helpless to stop it from happening. She had nothing. As hard as she searched her mind, Kip came up completely empty. "What are you doing, Cameron?"

"Sitting here."

"No. Really?" Kip said, getting irritated in spite of her best efforts. "What is this about?"

"I love you," he said, making it sound so simple. "And I love Jade. So here I am."

She wanted to stamp her feet and scream at the top of her lungs. Why was he so fucking stubborn? "Stop saying that.

You don't want me."

His face hardened. "If you ever tell me I don't want you again, I'll handcuff you to the bed and leave you there this time. I love you and I'm not fucking leaving this spot."

The front door opened and Josh walked in. Kip wanted to jump into his arms and beg him to rescue her. He glanced Cameron's way. Not an ounce of surprise marred Josh's features. He nodded.

"What's up?" Without waiting for a response, he disappeared inside his bedroom. She stared at the spot where he'd been, incapable of believing her eyes.

She crossed her arms over her chest and then uncrossed them when she realized what she'd done. There was a frown tugging at her brow but she couldn't stop it. When Kip couldn't take it any longer, she finally met Cameron's gaze. He smiled. A loud shriek rent the air, giving Kip hope she could escape. Josh's bedroom door opened.

"Monster alert. I've got it," he said, jogging down the hall.

Kip had already turned at the sound of Jade's cry and that's how Cameron got the drop on her. Snagging her from behind, he pulled her into his lap. His mouth covered hers and God help her, she let it happen. He tasted like ambrosia, like her dreams coming true. Her fingers brushed every inch of him she could reach, starving for any connection. She'd missed him so much. The idea she'd never touch him again in any way had almost killed her. Here he was, giving her another chance. She couldn't stop.

"Can't see a thing," Josh said, causing Kip to tear her mouth away.

He was covering Jade's eyes and keeping his gaze averted before disappearing inside his bedroom once more. The door closed with a definite snap. Cameron's chest shook beneath her. Feeling a bit shy, Kip turned her head, meeting his stare. The laughter and happiness in his eyes made her want to sigh.

"I don't want to leave here, Kip."

His admission caused her nose to sting. He meant it. She could see his heart.

"You and Jade mean everything to me. When you're not around, I can see all the pieces of me that are missing with a blinding clarity."

Kip held her breath. She felt the same. "I'm only whole when I'm with you."

"Just heading for the kitchen," Josh said, moving fast and still hiding Jade's eyes.

Kip pressed her forehead to Cameron's shoulder, hiding her smile. "Are you sure you want all this?"

His arms tightened around her. "You're not getting away from me. I'm serious. You're my home."

The pressure in her chest had nowhere to go. She loved this man. Straddling his hips, Kip kissed every exposed inch of skin she could find until Cameron was laughing so hard no sound emerged. When she had him where she wanted, Kip touched her head to his and stared into the slightly mismatched eyes that were only inches from her face.

"I love you, Cameron. So fucking much I can't catch my breath sometimes. If you ever leave me again, they'll never find your body."

Cameron released a happy sigh, warming her heart. "I wouldn't expect anything less."

*The End*

*Keep an eye out for the next No Rival,*

*Uncaged*

# Author Bio

*Charity Parkerson is an award winning and multi-published author with several companies. Born with no filter from her brain to her mouth, she decided to take this odd quirk and insert it in her characters.*

*\*2015 Readers' Favorite Award Winner*
*\*Winner of 2, 2014 Readers' Favorite Awards*
*\*2015 Passionate Plume Award Finalist*
*\*2013 Readers' Favorite Award Winner*
*\*2013 Reviewers' Choice Award Winner*
*\*2012 ARRA Finalist for Favorite Paranormal Romance*

*Five-time winner of The Mistress of the Darkpath*

*Connect with her online:*

*--Website: charityparkerson.com*
*--Facebook:*
*facebook.com/authorCharityParkerso*
*n*
*facebook.com/TheMenofSin*
*--Twitter: twitter.com/CharityParkerso*

www.ingramcontent.com/pod-product-compliance
Lightning Source LLC
Chambersburg PA
CBHW070750280626
47162CB00018B/2819